SCARED SILLY

CURSES ARE THE WORST

ELIZABETH EULBERG

SCHOLASTIC INC.

Copyright © 2023 by Elizabeth Eulberg, Inc.

All rights reserved. Published by Scholastic Inc., *Publishers since 1920*. SCHOLASTIC and associated logos are trademarks and/or registered trademarks of Scholastic Inc.

The publisher does not have any control over and does not assume any responsibility for author or third-party websites or their content.

No part of this publication may be reproduced, stored in a retrieval system, or transmitted in any form or by any means, electronic, mechanical, photocopying, recording, or otherwise, without written permission of the publisher. For information regarding permission, write to Scholastic Inc., Attention: Permissions Department, 557 Broadway, New York, NY 10012.

This book is a work of fiction. Names, characters, places, and incidents are either the product of the author's imagination or are used fictitiously, and any resemblance to actual persons, living or dead, business establishments, events, or locales is entirely coincidental.

ISBN 978-1-338-81535-1

10 9 8 7 6 5 4 3 2 1   23 24 25 26 27

Printed in the U.S.A.   40

First edition, March 2023

Book design by Stephanie Yang

FOR CECILIA AND RACHEL, THE FAIRY GOD*WITCHES*
OF CAULDRON'S COVE, WHO KEPT ME STOCKED
IN WITCHY PUNS. PINT OF ENCHANT-MINT
CHOCOLATE CHIP ICE CREAM ON ME!

WARNING!

According to Rule 1, section BOO!, paragraph yada yada of the *Publisher's Guide to Scaring Children*, I must warn you that the following story contains skin-crawling creatures and scary moments that would terrify even the bravest of souls.

What kind of scary things, you ask? Do you *really* want to know?

Oh, you do? Well, okay, then. (Pretty nosy if you ask me . . .)

We're talking blood, guts, *homework*, snotty tissues, kidnapping, *broccoli*, lightning, annoying *siblings*, a vat of goo, some dog poo (and the occasional rhyme from time to time), a *history* lesson, detention, *stinky cheese*, super long needles, and maybe worst of all . . . even more *broccoli*. Ewww.

Readers of this story may experience the following symptoms: being woken up in the middle of the night in a cold sweat, taco cravings, restless brain syndrome, suspicion of science teachers, need-to-read-under-a-blanket-itis, the sudden urge to hug your siblings, and the uncontrollable desire to keep turning the page.

It's probably best to put this book down and walk away. Pretend you never opened it and move on with your young, impressionable life.

However, if you think you're super, *duper* brave and want to continue, you're doing so at your own risk.

Wow, you think you're pretty tough, huh?

Impressive.

Fine, go ahead and read. Just don't say you weren't warned.

1

To begin our story, we need to travel back to over three hundred years ago. In the dark ages before indoor toilets and the internet. (Hey, you were warned things were going to get scary!)

In a time of witches. Yes, *witches*, as in rides-broomsticks-and-casts-spells witches. Now, not *all* had hairy moles on their cheeks, but since there was no running water, a lot of them smelled. But so did everybody else. Pretty much *everything* and *everyone* stank back then.

Okay, back to the witches.

Many had lived a quiet life until the Salem witch trials.

WARNING: HISTORY LESSON AHEAD! The following paragraph contains historical elements that may be considered "learning," but don't worry, this will be the last time it happens.

The Salem witch trials took place during the late 1600s in Massachusetts. Over two hundred people, mostly women, were accused of witchcraft or being possessed by the devil. It's also important to remember that back then, a woman who could read or solve equations was considered the devil's work. *A woman who can do math in the 1600s? She must be a witch! Burn her!* Anyhoo, hearings took place and nineteen people were executed by hanging.

Learning over. *Phew!*

Many witches fled Salem during this time, including Ann Wilder. Ann ended up in the small town of Cauldron's Cove. Because let's be real, if you name a town *Cauldron's Cove*, you're just asking for witches to flock there. It's like calling a town Bloodadelphia and not expecting vampires to move in. Because yes, vampires are also real, but that's a story for another time.

The townsfolk in Cauldron's Cove didn't trust this ginger-haired newcomer. Never trust a ginger—and I should know; I am one. One dark and stormy evening, a thunderstorm ravaged the town. A bolt of lightning caused the church to burn down. Without any proof, the town decided it was Ann's fault. The next night, the townspeople burned down Ann's house before burning *her* at the stake.

What a time to be alive, huh? *Yikes!*

As Ann was dragged up to the fiery pit, she screamed out to the crowd, "You hath underestimated my powers! Never underestimate a woman!" Then, with her final breath, Ann placed a curse upon the town.

Ann promised to release a series of creatures to terrorize the children and grandchildren of the townspeople. Because sometimes children have to pay for their parents' sins. And what would be more torturous for those responsible for her death than watching their children and grandchildren suffer?

But see, Ann really *was* bad at math. When you think about it, wouldn't you be, too? Remember, these were ye olden times when doing a little addition could make someone scream, *She's a witch!* So you couldn't blame a girl for not wanting to do her multiplication tables. (Although I highly recommend that you do *not* use the but-I-didn't-want-you-to-think-I-was-a-witch excuse for skipping your math homework. Believe me, I've tried, and it does *not* work.)

So yeah, Ann made a teeny-tiny error in her curse that caused it to be dormant for many, *many* years.

Three hundred and thirty-one years to be exact.

So instead of cursing the children and grandchildren of Ann's murderers, it's the great-great-great-great-great-great-great-great—*takes a deep breath*—great-great-grandchildren she cursed.

And now the time has come for Ann's monsters to be unleashed upon the unsuspecting children of Cauldron's Cove.

2

Fast-forward to the time of the internet, long hot showers, and flushing toilets. Looking at Cauldron's Cove now, one would think all Ann Wilder had cursed the town with was tourists.

Yes, the place that once trembled at the thought of witches now embraces them. Visitors are greeted with a WELCOME TO CAULDRON'S COVE! VISIT FOR A SPELL! sign with a cartoon picture of a witch on a broomstick. One can visit Witches' Way, the main street complete with a BLACK CAT CROSSING sign. It's populated with stores like the Warts and All Beauty Parlor, Arts & Witchcraft, Hocus Focus Photography Studio, and my personal favorite, Black Cat Creamery. Because who doesn't like a little Enchant-mint chocolate chip ice cream with a side of puns?

On weekends, tourists are treated to reenactments of witches around a cauldron and a magic show. Or they can visit the Haunted Museum or take a ride on a broom-shaped go-cart at Broom Broom Speedway.

Yet, with all the witchy stuff in town, there is not one mention of Ann Wilder and what the townspeople did to her all those years ago. It would probably be considered bad for business, what with the burning at the stake and curses and all. Instead, wouldn't you like to pick up some pumpkin bath salts at Bubble Bubble Toil and Trouble?

But all is not well in Cauldron's Cove.

I mean, of course something needs to be amiss or this wouldn't be that good of a book, huh?

It all started two nights ago when an unexpected thunderstorm came through town. Large hail rained down with booming lightning. Trees toppled. Power lines snapped. The town was in the dark for over twenty-four hours. School was even canceled.

Now, you may be thinking, *No school? Awesome!* But there is trouble brewing for the children of Cauldron's Cove. Not simply because school is back open. You see, no matter the century, decade, or day, adults will always try to make kids' lives miserable.

Let's look at the well-known torture device that is detention. No way did a kid come up with that. Especially at Cauldron's Cove Elementary School, where detention is in a tiny, cramped room that smells delightfully of stinky feet and moldy broccoli—not like regular broccoli smells good, am I right? (That's what you call a rhetorical question, which means you don't need to answer it because, *No duh*.)

But detention is exactly where ten-year-old Regan Charles finds herself. Regan knows a thing or two about disgusting smells. She's the oldest of five kids and has had to change plenty of super stinky, poopy diapers. She sits in the back corner and puts her hand up to cover her nose.

Regan nervously jitters her leg. She's going to be in so much trouble for getting detention.

She's not the only one.

"Just *relax*," Bennett Norland says as he walks into detention behind an annoyed Sofia Vargas.

Sofia stops in her tracks and turns to him, her light brown cheeks starting to turn crimson. "That's exactly what you said to me this morning before *you*"—she stabs Bennett in the chest with her index finger—"made us late for school."

"Whoa, whoa." Bennett holds his hands up in surrender. "Listen, sis—"

"I am *not* your sister!" she protests, even though in eighteen days, they'll technically be stepsiblings.

"—it's not my fault—"

"Of course, because nothing is ever *your* fault." Sofia throws her hands up in the air.

Bennett dribbles his basketball in reply. The dribbling or tossing of balls is not allowed out of gym, but the rules never seem to apply to Bennett.

"So let me make sure I've got this right," he begins. "A tree was blocking the road this morning because of the storm and caused us to be like one minute late—"

"Two minutes and fourteen seconds," Sofia corrects him.

"—and that's, like, somehow my fault?"

"You take forever in the bathroom!"

Bennett smooths down his perfectly coifed blond hair. "Hey, gotta look good for the ladies."

"*Please*. Your ego is going to cause me to vomit all over this already disgusting room."

Sofia sits at the desk closest to the window . . . until Bennett plops down next to her. Then she moves back a row.

Regan uncomfortably shifts in her seat. The two have yet to acknowledge her. Even though Regan is quiet, she's kind of hard to miss. She's wearing a bright blue floral dress; her red hair stands out in the drab white cinder block room. And well, Regan isn't exactly small. Some people even tease her and call her fat, but she doesn't care because she *is* fat.

Besides, why should anyone have to apologize for taking up space?

"I can't believe I'm here," Sofia says in utter disbelief.

To be honest, I don't really believe it, either.

Sofia Vargas in detention?

Okay, you don't really know Sofia that well yet, but let me tell you that she is a legend at the school. She's *that* student. The one that gets straight As. The one teachers will leave in charge if they need to step out. The one who is in fifth grade even though she's nine, because she skipped second grade. The one who gets called on even if she doesn't raise her hand because everybody—including the teachers—knows Sofia will always have the correct answer.

And between you and me, she's pretty insufferable about it.

Bennett kicks his feet up on his desk. "Oh, *relax.*"

The pencil in Sofia's hand snaps in two.

Bennett continues, ignoring Sofia's glare. "It's just an hour of your precious time. You'll probably even get to do homework. So what's the difference between being here and at your desk at home?"

"I can't believe my father is going to marry your mother," Sofia says with a scowl.

"Believe it, sis," Bennett replies with a wink.

"Ah, hello?" Standing at the doorway is another stranger to detention: Darius Washington. He looks down at a piece of paper in his hand. "Is this detention?"

"Sadly," Sofia replies.

"Really?" Darius looks at Sofia, clearly confused.

"Yes, Darius. I'm sitting at a desk in detention, so I'm here." Sofia jerks her chin accusingly at Bennett.

"Oh, okay." Darius takes off his Black Panther backpack that's decorated with different comic book buttons. "I've never been before."

"Neither have we," Bennett replies. "I mean, honestly, we were only a little late because of the storm, but Ms. Stein stopped us when we arrived and gave us detention. How unfair is that?"

Darius nods along. "Yeah, I was reading a comic book on my way to class. I just got to an epic battle scene, and suddenly Ms. Stein takes it out of my hand and gives me detention!"

This gets Sofia to sit up straighter in her seat. "You shouldn't have been given detention for reading in the hallway. It's allowed in the rules."

And Sofia would know. She's read the school handbook. All 112 pages. She even submitted a list of grammatical corrections to the principal, although he has yet to respond to her *two* follow-up emails about it.

How rude.

"Yeah, it seemed weird, but it's not like I could argue with a teacher," Darius replies with a shrug.

"You know, we shouldn't be here, either," Bennett says. "A few of my buddies were also late this morning, and *they* didn't get in trouble. The whole town is still a mess after that storm. It's not our fault we're late." He shoots a look at Sofia. "And it's certainly not mine."

Bennett finally turns to acknowledge Regan. "What brought you in? Were you late this morning, too?"

It takes a minute for Regan to realize Bennett is talking to her. "Oh!" She shakes her head. "No."

"Reading?" Darius throws out.

"No."

"Well, then?" Bennett presses.

Regan looks down at the desk, feeling foolish. "I don't know."

"What do you mean, *you don't know*?" Bennett snorts. "I mean, you *have* to know why you're here."

"That's just it; I didn't do anything." Regan bites the corner of her lip.

Okay, you know how some people say they didn't do something, like break a glass or talk in class, even though they positively, absolutely did it. (I'm not saying *you* would ever do anything like that, just other people.)

Well, Regan *is* telling the truth. She didn't do anything to get into detention.

Not like Sofia, Bennett, and Darius deserve to be there, either.

So yeah, this seems pretty fishy, huh?

Sofia turns around in her desk to stare at Regan. "What happened *exactly*?"

"I was walking down the hallway and Ms. Stein told me I had to report to detention."

"And you didn't think to ask why?"

Regan slumps down in her seat. "Well, I didn't want to cause any trouble."

Here's something you should know about Regan Charles: She likes to make life easier for others. This includes not arguing with her teachers or parents. It's not as if Regan is happy to be in detention. The last thing she needs is to spend an hour here after school given all that she has to do. She helps out at her parents' Bed and Boofast, yet another Cauldron's Cove tourist spot. She makes beds and arranges the welcome baskets for guests—and this is on top of helping with her four siblings. She has to get Roman and Rylee back and forth to school and make sure they finish their homework. Then at night she helps with River and Rose: baths and pajamas. Not to mention the fact that it always takes Regan much longer to do homework with her learning differences.

So when Ms. Stein told Regan to report to detention, she just did what she was told, even though something in her gut told her it wasn't right.

Darius glances at the door. "Okay, I thought it was odd when I was sent here for reading, but *that* makes no sense. None."

"Unless she's not telling the truth." Sofia looks at Regan skeptically.

Heat rushes to Regan's pale white cheeks. She has no trouble being the center of attention at home, but in school it's different. "Why would I lie?" she says, her voice barely audible.

Sofia narrows her eyes at Regan, who turns her attention to the graffiti on top of the desk.

Darius glances at the door. "Have you guys noticed anything different about Ms. Stein today?"

Bennett slaps his hand on the desk. "Yes! See, none of us deserve to be in detention. When Ms. Stein gets here, we should tell her—"

"Tell me what?"

Uh-oh. Busted.

Because at the entrance of the door stands the infamous Ms. Stein.

Well, she's not infamous yet, but she will be soon.

Just you wait.

The aforementioned science teacher walks into the room, an unsettling smile on her face as she takes in the four students in front of her.

"Please continue, Bennett. What did you want to tell me?" Ms. Stein says it like a dare.

All of Bennett's earlier bravado deflates like a balloon. "Ah, nothing."

Remember before when Darius said Ms. Stein is acting different? I mean, it was just on the last page, so I'm sure you do. See, here's the deal with Ms. Stein: She's one of the friendliest and most likeable teachers at school. She's just a few years out of college and always decorates her room with bright colors and tries to make science fun. She even once staged a fake murder and left clues for the students to figure out who dun it. How cool is that? (Not cool to some parents, but then again, some parents are just *not cool*. But if your parents bought you this book, then they are super-duper cool. Like the *coolest*.)

While Ms. Stein is a good teacher, something is definitely off today. Her long curly black hair is in a messy bun, there are deep purple circles under her eyes, and she seems completely frazzled. As in hasn't-slept-in-years-and-drank-a-zillion-Cherry-Cokes frazzled. As in really-needs-to-pee-but-there-is-no-bathroom-for-miles frazzled.

So yeah, not good.

And that weird feeling in Regan's gut? There's another reason for it: Ms. Stein was scanning the hallway and smiled the second she saw Regan, like she'd been waiting for her. She looked almost gleeful when she gave Regan detention, like she was looking for any excuse to get Regan into this room.

Or maybe Regan is just being paranoid.

(She's not.)

Ms. Stein puts a large black satchel on top of the desk and pulls out a leather notebook. A manic smile settles on her face as she stares at the cover. She presses the notebook against her chest, hugging it tightly. She looks out to the four students in front of her. "Well, well, well . . . An important lesson for you, children: Never underestimate a woman. It's finally time. Here we all are. And so it begins."

Never underestimate a woman. While completely and utterly true, where have we heard that before?

So yeah, things are not looking good for these four students.

3

Here's something else you should know about Regan: She does not like creepy things.

She's not Darius, who has read all The Walking Dead, Tales from the Crypt, *and* Swamp Thing comics. Usually *before* bed.

The undead? Blood? Guts? Running for your life?

Nope. Not something Regan likes to read—or even think—about. (It's going to be a rough time for poor Regan.)

But even Darius looks uncomfortable with the expression on Ms. Stein's face right now. She has this look like she's . . . hungry.

Although, let's be fair, who isn't a bit peckish after school?

Darius reaches into his backpack and pulls out a container with freshly baked fudgy brownies. He places one of the brownies on top of his desk and pushes it forward.

"Um, Ms. Stein," Darius starts. "Would you like a brownie?"

Ms. Stein ignores Darius and instead flips through the notebook in her hand.

So yeah, that's not normal behavior. *Who turns down a brownie?* I wouldn't trust anybody who can say no to such a delicious treat. I'd certainly not want to be stuck in a tiny, smelly room with them.

"Yes, yes, yes . . ." Ms. Stein says to herself as she scans quickly through the notebook pages. Then she reaches into her large satchel and pulls out a box of tissues, a long wooden black pepper grinder, a pack of gum, and . . . a tiny kitten?

This perks Regan up. She loves cats and dogs and everything fuzzy and furry. Maybe detention won't be so bad if she gets to play with a cute, cuddly kitten.

Suddenly, Ms. Stein's head snaps up to the students. "I have an assignment for you."

Bennett groans, while Sofia has her pen at the ready, because of course she does. Since Regan has never been in detention—and oh, is she going to hear about this when she gets home—she isn't sure what to expect. She didn't realize there was going to be even *more* work to do.

Detention *and* extra homework? And she still doesn't know why she's here!

So. Not. Fair.

But even I have to admit the items Ms. Stein has pulled out are kind of intriguing. Maybe they're going to do some kind of cool science experiment?

Instead, Ms. Stein marches up to Darius with the black-and-white kitten squirming in her hand. Darius leans away.

A smile spreads on Ms. Stein's face as she thrusts the kitten at Darius. "Hold this."

"Oh, but I'm really allergic and—" Darius begins, but Ms. Stein has already turned her back on him.

The kitten responds by clawing at Darius's shirt. He holds the kitten as far away from his face as possible, but it's too late. Darius's eyes are watering and his nose starts to twitch.

"I really can't—" Darius stops as the beginning of a major, snotty sneeze works its way to his nose.

But Ms. Stein's focus is now on Bennett. She holds out the packet of gum. "Would you like some?"

Bennett shrugs before popping a piece of gum into his mouth.

Huh. Darius gets to hold a kitten and Bennett gets to chew gum. Maybe detention isn't *that* bad.

Ms. Stein paces around the room before settling in front of Sofia. She holds out the black pepper grinder and starts grinding pepper on the surface of Sofia's desk. The little black flakes cover Sofia's neatly arranged desktop.

Okay, *this* right here isn't normal science teacher behavior.

Sofia, however, doesn't appear confused. "I'm assuming we're doing an experiment on the surface tension of water. Where's the soap?"

"No," Ms. Stein bluntly replies as she turns to Regan.

The only sound echoing in the tiny room is the click-click-clicking of Regan's desk as her knee bounces a million miles a minute.

The corner of Ms. Stein's lip curls up, like she's enjoying how nervous she's making Regan.

That uneasy feeling grows in Regan's stomach. There is no way that this can be good.

(Spoiler alert: It isn't.)

Regan's shoulders tighten as Ms. Stein walks behind her. Then Ms. Stein picks up a few strands of Regan's red hair. She slowly curls them around her finger.

Then she yanks. *Hard.*

"Ow!" Regan cries out as she grabs the back of her head. Her eyes burn from the pain of having some of her hair ripped from her head.

Can you believe a teacher just did that?

Regan opens her mouth to protest and demand to see the principal. But then she quickly closes it. It could get her in even more trouble.

So instead, Regan stays quiet.

Now it's Sofia who is squirming in her seat. She's leaning away from the black pepper on her desk, rubbing her nose. "Ms. Stein, I'm afraid if we aren't—*ah, ah*—"

Like a magician, Ms. Stein produces a tissue a second before Sofia lets out a huge sneeze.

"Wonderful!" Ms. Stein exclaims. She picks up Sofia's tissue and *looks inside* at the mucusy mess left behind.

Gross.

"As for your assignment," Ms. Stein continues as she walks back to the front of the room, "you are each to write an essay on what you believe makes you special as a member of the *student body* at Cauldron's Cove Elementary."

Bennett lets out a little laugh. "That'll be easy." He then leans back and puts his hands behind his head.

One thing you need to know about Bennett Norland is that he's one of those dudes who just seem to breeze by in school. Not a care in the world, this kid. But he's also so chill and totally nonthreatening that it's kinda hard not to like him. *Unless* you're Sofia, that is.

Ms. Stein holds out the palm of her hand in front of Bennett. "There is absolutely no gum in detention."

"But you—" Bennett starts before Ms. Stein cuts him off.

"Spit it out." She points at her palm. "*Now.*"

Um, how unfair is that? It was Ms. Stein who offered Bennett the gum. But alas, Bennett takes out the pink wad of gum covered in his slobber and places it directly in Ms. Stein's palm. Who, in turn, smiles even though Bennett basically just hocked a loogie in her hand.

Barf.

And then, because things aren't weird enough, Ms. Stein places Bennett's gum, Sofia's tissue, and Regan's hair in their own plastic bags.

Nothing to worry about here!

The kitten Darius has been holding starts to wiggle out of his grasp. "Ah!" he calls out before pulling it closer to his chest. He blinks back tears and does his best to fight back the mega mucus that's currently clogging up his nose.

(Spoiler alert: Darius is about to lose the epic booger battle.)

"Need a tissue?" Ms. Stein holds out a tissue box to Darius like she could read his mind.

Ms. Stein trades the kitten for a tissue. Once the tissue is in his hand, Darius lets out the biggest, snottiest sneeze of his life.

And then another one.

And another.

"Marvelous!" Ms. Stein exclaims before—are you ready for this?— she holds out her hand for Darius's snot-drenched tissue.

Let's just hope Ms. Stein also has some hand sanitizer in that big bag of hers, because *yuck*.

Sofia raises her hand. "Ms. Stein, is there a word count requirement for this assignment?"

Regan groans to herself. Her head hurts from the whole *having her hair ripped from her head* and now she has to write an *essay*.

"The assignment?" Ms. Stein repeats like she's confused. "Oh, yes, the assignment, right! What makes *you* special."

"What makes us special?" Darius says as he sniffles.

Since you don't really know Darius that well yet, let's take a look at what *does* makes Darius special. He isn't a brainiac like Sofia or a jock like Bennett. He does like to bake. Yes, as in cinnamon-spiced cupcakes and pumpkin scones baking. As in the aforementioned fudgy brownies, which he made last night. *Boys can bake, too, you know!* He also has a close group of friends. They usually spend time after school in his tree house reading comics or watching Marvel movies. They even started creating their own comic book characters, hybrids between their favorite superheroes and scary creatures called Marvelous Monsters. Darius sort of oversees it, while his buddies Javier and Cole write with him and Keenan draws.

But that doesn't really make him special at *school*. He isn't in any clubs. He's a decent student. That's what, three sentences? Maybe he can stretch it out to four. Maybe.

Not like it's hard to stretch something out. Like a sentence. You could rewrite a sentence a few times saying the same thing. You just need to use different words. Break the thesaurus out. It's possible to say something in more than one way. It's also conceivable to portray a scenario through multiple avenues. Just like it's doable to convey a sentiment by various means.

You get the idea or, one could say, *the gist*.

Ms. Stein's eyes settle on Darius. "Your essay is to be two pages, single spaced, at least five hundred words."

Five hundred words?

Uh-oh.

Regan is about to raise her hand and ask if she could have more time. She's usually allowed to have different deadlines with her learning differences. But she's scared to draw any more attention to herself. She likes her hair and would like to keep it, *thankyouverymuch*.

"Any questions?" Ms. Stein walks abruptly to the door before waiting for a response. "I'll be back. You have an hour to complete this assignment, but remember: I've got my eyes on you. *All of you*."

Then she lets out a laugh. One that causes shivers in all four students.

And not a that's-so-funny laugh. A you-have-no-idea-what-you're-in-for laugh.

Because they have *no idea* what they are in for.

Ms. Stein gives them one more unsettling look before leaving them alone in the room.

What are they supposed to do now?

Bennett smirks. "So do you think I can just write my name five hundred times, because there's nobody like me at this school?"

"Your ego alone would certainly take up more than two pages," Sofia fires back before she starts writing furiously in her notebook.

Bennett leans over to her, and she scoots her desk back. "Hey, Sof."

"It's Sofia."

"I'll do dishes for a whole week if you write mine."

"No."

Meanwhile, Regan is staring down at the blank piece of paper with dread.

"Okay, seriously, what was that?" Darius asks as he takes off his Black Panther (more like black-and-white kitten at this point) sweatshirt, revealing a Captain America T-shirt underneath.

"The assignment?" Sofia asks.

"Ah, *no*. I can't be the only one who thinks that whole . . . scene was weird. The gum, the pepper, the kitten, the hair . . . None of this

27

makes sense. Us being in detention. Regan doesn't even know why she's here! And then Ms. Stein is collecting dirty tissues, Regan's hair, and Bennett's gum, and . . . I mean, *come on*."

Darius stops talking and looks hopefully over at Sofia, since she seems to know everything. And goodness, does she like to tell people when she's right. And annoyingly, she's always right.

And super, super smug about it.

Sofia sighs. "Let's just do what we're told so we can get out of here. Not like I'll ever be able to get the stench of this room out of my mind." Her nose twitches up. "Or my clothes."

"Oh, come on, Sof," Bennett begins.

"It's Sofia." She glares at Bennett. "Although nothing can compare to how stinky you are."

"Hey, I've gotten no complaints." Bennett flashes Sofia an arrogant smile. "It's called Eau de Stud."

"*You're* called a doofus."

Bennett puts his hand over his heart like he's wounded. "Aw, that hurts, sis."

"I am *not* your sister."

"Soon, very soon." Then Bennett mimics Ms. Stein's cackle.

Sofia clenches her jaw as she continues to write.

Meanwhile, Regan's still staring at the pen in her hand as if she's willing it to magically write her essay.

"Hey, Regan, you okay over there?" Darius asks.

Regan nods. "Yeah, I guess. I'm just not sure what to write."

"Me too," Darius confesses as he gives Regan a reassuring smile.

Which Regan appreciates, since she's about to burst into tears.

When you think about it, who could blame her? Wouldn't *you* be upset if you didn't know why you were put in detention? Not to mention, you know, the whole hair pulling.

"Can we all be quiet so we can finish the assignment?" Sofia says so sternly, everybody stops talking.

The only sound in the room is that of pencils and pens being dragged across paper and Regan's jittering knee.

Truth be told, all four students do try their best with their essays, even Bennett.

Do you want to know what they write about?

Oh, you do? My, my, my, you *are* quite nosy, aren't you? We're going to get along very well, you and me.

Sofia's is not surprisingly filled with facts: Her standing in classes, her recent test scores. She's even included a chart.

Since "Because I'm Bennett Norland" is only four words long,

Bennett has written about his athletic talents and—this is a direct quote—"I don't want to brag, but people just like me. That's not having a big ego, it's just a fact, you know?"

Darius focuses on his friends and spends most of the time talking about how they make the school special. He ends with, "A school isn't just about one person. It's built around an entire community." He's a good one, that Darius.

After much, *much* deliberation, Regan starts off her essay detailing that she's not a good student, but she tries. Which is true. There's probably nobody at the school who works harder than Regan. She writes about her two younger siblings who also attend Cauldron's Cove Elementary. How Regan brings them to school, and often makes their lunches, since her parents are busy with their popular bed-and-breakfast in addition to running after her other much younger siblings. And in a somewhat heartbreaking way, she ends with, "While I don't have the ~~brians~~ smarts like some people, I like to think I add a little bit of kindness to this school."

Which is *exactly* why Regan was sent to detention.

She doesn't know this yet.

But she soon will.

After what seems like an eternity to the students—but in reality is exactly sixty minutes after detention started—Ms. Stein enters the room. She picks up each of the pieces of paper and quickly reads through them.

"No, no, no!" Ms. Stein shouts. Her hands slam down on the front desk, which causes the students to jump. "This is not good enough! I need more speci—" She clears her throat. "You all need to come back tomorrow."

"What?" Sofia protests. "Section two, paragraph F of the school manual—"

"I don't care what the manual says. I am not done with you yet."

No, Ms. Stein isn't done with Sofia, Bennett, Darius, and Regan.

In fact, their punishment is just beginning.

4

Here's something you probably already figured out: Bennett Norland is one calm, cool, and collected guy. Emphasis on the *cool*, obviously.

Yeah, Bennett isn't the type of dude to let things get to him.

So then, why exactly is he biking past Ms. Stein's house after hanging with his boys?

Hmmm. That's not on Bennett's way home. Should we see what he's up to?

Yes? Oh, you like to spy on people, too? I really do think this is the start of a beautiful friendship.

I don't know about you, but I agree with Bennett when he said this whole Ms. Stein thing is so not fair. Why Bennett? Why any of them? His buddies Max and Jimmy and Stu were also late this morning, but they didn't get in trouble. Then Ms. Stein got mad at Bennett for chewing the gum that *she* gave him?

Not cool. And the thing is, Ms. Stein usually *is* cool, as much as a science teacher can be.

Could this be punishment for Bennett screaming "It's alive! *IT'S ALIVE!*" last week in class when they used a potato to power a light bulb? Everybody laughed. *Everybody*, even Ms. Stein.

Something isn't right.

So perhaps that's why Bennett is outside Ms. Stein's house.

What does Bennett expect to find? you may be asking. Good question. You really are quite clever, aren't you? Especially since you have excellent taste in reading material, if I do say so myself.

I usually know everything, but even *I* don't know what Bennett expects to find. It's not like Ms. Stein will have a sign in her yard that says I GOT SOME BAD NEWS AND I AM NOT HANDLING IT WELL. SOME MAY EVEN SAY I'M QUITE MAD. MY BAD.

But then again, things always have a way of working out for Bennett. He's just a lucky guy.

But I can assure you, dear reader, his luck will soon run out.

And as luck will have it, something *is* going on at Ms. Stein's. The two-story house has all the lights off outside and the curtains drawn, but there are lights flashing that can be seen pulsating throughout the whole house.

One might guess she has the TV on, but in every room?

Just what exactly *is* Ms. Stein up to?

Bennett jumps off his bike and parks it behind a tree that had fallen over during the storm. He hunches down as he carefully approaches Ms. Stein's house. He tries to peek through a crack in the drapes but has to hold his hands up to his eyes, as it's incredibly bright.

He moves to another window, trying to see inside, but the light's still too intense.

Bennett rounds the corner to the back. There's a one-inch gap in the drapes, and he's able to get a glimpse inside of what appears to be Ms. Stein's dining room. In the center is a dining table that has a large metal ball, which has bursts of lightning radiating from it. At least it looks like lightning. Even though that's impossible, right? Little green glowing vials of what is best described as goo (and yes, that's a scientific term, *goo*) are lined on top of the table, next to some knives and large needles. You know, typical dining room décor. The room is littered with notes and drawings. Next to the table is a very large item covered in a blanket.

I don't know what it's like inside *your* home, but I'd say this is a very odd dining room indeed.

Bennett presses his nose against the glass.

At that precise moment, another set of eyes appears in front of him.

Busted!

Bennett stumbles back. What excuse is he going to use to explain to Ms. Stein why he's there?

But as the figure pulls back the curtain, it isn't Ms. Stein.

Bennett's eyes grow wide in horror.

The person staring back at him is someone who . . . no, it can't be . . .

Bennett is looking at . . . another Bennett.

~~~~~~~~

"Sofia! Sofia!" Bennett bursts into their house a few minutes later, sweat dripping down his face.

He finds his future stepsister sitting at the kitchen table with her homework spread out.

"I was just—I can't believe—" He bends down, trying to catch his breath. "You're never going to—"

"Just relax," Sofia replies to him with an eye roll.

"Sof!"

"It's Sofia."

"I was just at Ms. Stein's and there was lightning inside her dining room and a table with all this green junk and knives, and then there was me! I was in there, staring back at me! It was me!" He takes a deep breath.

Sofia's reply is to yawn, because of course it is.

"Did you hear me?" Bennett's basically screaming at this point.

Sofia scowls at him. "And here I assumed you were very familiar with your reflection, Bennett."

"But it wasn't my reflection! It was me! I mean, it wasn't really me. But like . . ."

What exactly did Bennett see? It *wasn't* him. No, this dude was the same height, had Bennett's eyes and hair and face, but he was a little . . . off. He looked greenish. And his features weren't as defined as Bennett's. He was like a blurry version of Bennett. And he had this ridiculous look on his face, like he was about to let out a huge fart, and Bennett has never, ever looked that silly.

Of course, Bennett *has* passed gas. Everybody has. You, your parents, your teacher, this writer . . .

Sofia lets out an annoyed sigh. "What's your point?"

"*My point?* My point is that Ms. Stein is doing some weird stuff in her house, and, like . . ."

"Let me make sure I have this correct," Sofia starts, without taking her eyes off the math book in front of her. "You're saying that our science teacher has cloned you?"

Bennett stares back at her. *A clone?* Is that what Bennett saw? Is that even possible?

"Um, yeah?" Bennett replies, but not with much confidence.

Sofia shakes her head. "Once again, your ego never fails to amaze me."

"But, Sof!"

"It's Sofia."

Bennett lets out a frustrated groan. "*Sofia*, I can't believe you don't believe me. I *know* what I saw."

"Are you letting my dad's calendar of events get to you?"

Oh, here's something you should know about Sofia's father: He runs Cauldron's Cove Visitors Center. With Halloween next month, he has flyers around the house for all the upcoming activities, like a Haunted House Tour, a Zombie 5K, a Witches' Brew Festival, and more. One could get a little carried away with so many spooky events planned, but in Bennett's defense, there isn't anything on the calendar that has to do with clones.

"Come on, sis—"

"I am *not* your sister."

"Ugh!" Bennett throws his hands up. "Never mind!"

Poor Bennett. If his future stepsister, who personally witnessed how odd Ms. Stein was behaving today, didn't believe him, who would?

Perhaps what Bennett needs is some proof.

5

Let's be real for a second, shall we? Not like I've been holding back on you.

Here's the thing: Not everybody likes school. I know, *shocking*! There are some students—very few and far between and not you or me or anybody you may associate with—who dread school.

For Regan, it's not like she doesn't like school, it's just hard for her. There are a lot of classes that make Regan anxious. Usually, math and reading are at the top of the list of Regan's I-Hope-I-Don't-Make-a-Fool-Out-of-Myself Classes. But as she arrives at school the next day, there is one class she is dreading the most.

And it's not because she's worried about slipping up and saying the wrong thing. Or getting something jumbled in her head.

Nope. That stuff is nothing compared to what she's afraid is waiting for her in Ms. Stein's science class.

Regan cautiously walks into class after lunch. She sits up in the front like she always does so she can concentrate. With her auditory-processing issues, she can easily forget what is said aloud or get confused, so she takes lots of notes. Even if she gets teased about it by some of the boys in class.

Boys. Am I right?

Now, not all boys are bad. For real. If the person who is reading this now is a boy, you are clearly a good one with excellent taste in books. You probably don't smell too bad, either. *Probably*.

Anyhoo, here's another good guy now.

Darius walks into class with his buddies Keenan and Javier, laughing like he doesn't have a care in the world. As the rest go to the back of the room, Darius pauses in front of Regan. "Hey, how are you doing?"

For a beat Regan looks around, wondering who Darius is talking to. Regan isn't the kind of person people check in on. Especially her fellow classmates.

Darius glances over his shoulder for a beat before he leans in. "That was weird yesterday and I've been kind of dreading this class all day."

"Me too," Regan admits with a small smile. It's nice to have someone get how she feels.

"And I'm in so much trouble with my mom for having to go back today. It's not right."

Regan nods along because it *isn't* right. At all.

First, she gets in trouble for . . . no reason at all. Yet nobody believes her, especially her parents. They were so upset that they had to find someone to pick up Roman and Rylee after school today, since Regan will still be stuck in detention. The B&B is fully booked for most of the fall, so they've been extra busy. In fact, they didn't even react when Regan told them that Ms. Stein yanked out some of her hair. It was like they thought Regan wasn't telling the truth. Regan touches the back of her head now, remembering how much it hurt.

There's the physical pain of having hair ripped from her head, but then there's the emotional pain of letting her family down. Of not being believed. And well, that stung a whole lot more.

But Darius believes Regan. He was there. He knows.

"Have you seen Bennett today?" Darius asks as he leans against Regan's desk. Regan can't help but notice how people are looking at them curiously.

Maisy Menzel (who you should know is one of the most popular girls in class and has the lead in all the musicals and was even featured in Cauldron's Cove Halloween musical last year . . . so yeah, she's *that girl*) walks by and glares at Regan when she notices Darius talking to her. She whispers something to the clones that always follow her around and they all giggle.

Regan sinks in her seat as Darius continues, oblivious to the whispers that are starting around class. "Yeah, Bennett looks super stressed and paranoid. Like he's seen a ghost. It seems like we aren't the only ones rattled by yesterday."

"Really?" It makes Regan feel a little better if always-super-cool Bennett also got freaked out. In fact, just having Darius talk to her helps block out all the stares. Regan turns in her seat so she can no longer see Maisy pushing her nose up and snorting like a pig. (Ugh, bullies are the *worst*. Well, maybe not the worst thing that's going to happen to poor Regan today.) "I had history with Sofia this morning and she seemed fine."

"Of course she did," Darius says with a shake of his head.

Regan can't help but laugh even though there's something you should know about Regan: She's a little scared of Sofia. Probably not shocking given Sofia's not-so-sunny disposition, but Sofia is so smart, it makes Regan feel extra self-conscious. She tries to avoid speaking around Sofia if she can help it. But then there's a part of Regan that feels sorry for Sofia.

Why?

Well, here's something sad you should know about Sofia: Her mother died when Sofia was only five years old. Regan frowns thinking about how hard that must've been. Regan's family is her whole life, and she couldn't imagine if anything happened to one of her parents or siblings.

She swallows the sadness down. The last thing she wants to do is start crying around Darius. He'll never come over and talk to her again.

Darius looks at the classroom door with a frown. "I should probably sit down before Ms. Stein gets here. Catch you later." He gives her a nod with his chin before settling down with his buddies.

Regan finds herself sitting a bit straighter. Yeah, she's nervous about what's going to happen when Ms. Stein walks in and later at detention, but she's not alone in it. She has Darius. And maybe even Bennett.

The talking in the room quiets when Ms. Stein hurries into class, looking even worse than yesterday. Her clothes are wrinkled, like she slept in them, but it's pretty clear from her bloodshot eyes that she hasn't slept at all.

Ms. Stein sits down at her desk without acknowledging the students in front of her. Instead, she opens up her notebook and starts flipping through it. "Yes . . . yes . . ." she says under her breath.

Regan and her fellow classmates look around in confusion. It's like Ms. Stein hasn't even realized class has started.

A minute goes by.

Two minutes . . .

The class is eerily silent. The only noise comes from Ms. Stein flipping through her notebook. Regan can't decide if this silence is worse than Maisy Menzel's mean murmuring before class.

Let's be real: Neither is great.

Ms. Stein grabs her messy hair as she leans down and starts jotting notes. And keeps writing. And writing.

Five minutes have passed in class . . .

Someone in the back of the room coughs.

Ms. Stein's head snaps up, a startled look on her face as she sees thirty students staring back at her. Then her eyes settle on Regan and a slow, mischievous smile spreads on her face.

"Well, hello, children. I'm busy preparing for a very big experiment." She then licks her lips. "Very big indeed."

A chill goes down Regan's spine. She resists glancing back at Darius.

"So today you are going to watch a movie," Ms. Stein continues, to the delight of the class.

As the lights go down, Regan can't pay attention to the documentary

43

on insects. She's too busy focusing on Ms. Stein and her manic energy. Scribbling in her notebook. Talking to herself. A few times she lets out a cackle.

BRRRRRRING!

Regan nearly jumps out of her skin as the alarm rings signaling the end of the period. She quickly gathers her things and wants nothing more than to get out of the classroom.

"Regan, Darius," Ms. Stein calls out. "A moment, please."

Regan stops in her tracks, her shoulders automatically tensing. She turns around to find Darius looking a little sick to his stomach.

"Please, come here." She motions to the front of her desk. She snaps her notebook shut and puts it in her drawer before standing up. "I hope you're both ready for detention later."

"Yes, ma'am," Darius replies with a nervous waver in his voice.

Ms. Stein looks at Regan. She reaches out and twirls a strand of Regan's hair around her finger. "And you?"

"Ah—" The words are stuck in Regan's throat as she prepares for more hair to be yanked. "Yes."

"Splendid!" Ms. Stein releases Regan's hair. "I have so much planned for you. You're going to be part of something truly amazing."

"Um, okay," Darius says as he takes a step closer to the door. "Should we get a pass or . . ."

"You may leave, but remember, children, sometimes the ultimate sacrifice needs to be made for the greater good."

Wait. What does that mean?

"See you soon." Then Ms. Stein lets out another cackle.

Darius grabs Regan's elbow as he exits the classroom. She follows him, grateful for his guidance as she felt frozen in place.

"What do you think that was all about?" Darius asks as soon as they're in the clear. "Ultimate sacrifice? That's stuff heroes say before they do something that gets them killed saving the world."

Regan can only nod in reply. She doesn't even know how she'll be able to concentrate in her next class, which is her hardest: math. She's just . . . you know what, I promised you I wasn't going to hold back. So here's the deal: Regan is utterly terrified. None of this makes sense. Ms. Stein seems threatening, and it's just not good! Nope, Regan does not like this at all.

Do you blame the girl?

"I don't think we should show up for detention," Darius suggests. "I've got a bad feeling about it."

As much as Regan agrees with Darius, she thinks about what

would happen if she didn't go to detention. "I know, but I'm already in so much trouble, skipping detention would just . . ." Regan shakes her head. "Ms. Stein is our teacher. She's probably just overwhelmed. I'm sure it'll be fine."

Even as those words leave Regan's mouth, she knows it's not true.

(Spoiler alert: It isn't.)

6

Now, when you really think about it, does anybody look forward to detention?

Of course not!

But as Bennett said yesterday, there's no one like him at school. Because Bennett can't wait to get into detention. He practically drags Sofia into the gross, stinky room after school.

Darius and Regan arrive a few minutes later, both looking unsettled.

"Hey, everybody ready for this?" Darius asks the group, but Sofia simply ignores him, while Bennett is too busy with his eyes focused on the teacher's desk in front. Regan is sitting in the back with her shoulders slumped.

Ms. Stein walks in with her big black bag slung around her shoulder. She plunks it down with a thud on the desk, then takes out a box of tissues and places it front and center.

Darius shifts uncomfortably next to Bennett. Regan places her hand on the back of her still-sore head. Sofia has her notebook out, her pen in its usual position, poised to take notes.

Ms. Stein claps impatiently. "We've got lots of work to do today, children. Yesterday almost worked, but I need more from you. And I don't want to waste any more time. We've already had to wait over three hundred years."

The four students all exchange confused glances.

Three hundred years? What happened three hundred years ago?

Why, I believe that was the ye olde smelly times referred to in the first chapter. There was something about a thing that sounds like the Schmalem schmitch schmiles.

Yep. You know, dear reader. And you also know this can't be good.

Ms. Stein continues, "But we must soldier on. I finally have—" She lets out a yelp of annoyance. "I forgot one thing. Stay right there. Don't move a muscle! Soon, we will begin."

She rushes out of the room, the click-clack of her heels receding down the hallway.

But guess what? Ms. Stein left her bag behind.

Remember when I said that Bennett is just a lucky guy? Well, would you look at that. Bennett needs proof, right? And what better proof than the notebook Ms. Stein keeps scribbling in and reading. It's probably Ms. Stein's diary. There has to be something inside that he can use. Or at least an explanation for what's going on.

Girls and their secrets, am I right?

Bennett jumps up and goes through Ms. Stein's bag.

"What are you doing?" Sofia hisses at him.

Bennett starts pulling out the items crammed inside Ms. Stein's bag: More tissues, tweezers, a feather, and a blanket covered in some kind of hair.

Darius leans back in his chair, his nose already twitching.

Bennett's eyes get wide. "Ah . . ."

Then he pulls out a huge needle. He clinks it on the wooden desk.

"What—what—what is that for?" Regan can barely squeak out.

Bennett gags as he reaches in and holds up a bag filled with dark liquid.

"Is that . . . *blood*?" Darius asks as he moves his desk away from the contents of the bag. "Okay, seriously, Ms. Stein was off today in class and saying crazy stuff. We really should—"

"Finally!" Bennett exclaims. "I think this might give us some answers to what's going on and what all this stuff is for." Bennett places the notebook on the top of his desk and the others can't help but get up from their desks and gather cautiously around. It's a black leather-bound notebook. On the front, written in silver pen with shaky handwriting, it reads:

The Journal of Victoria Francesca Stein.

7

You don't need to be a genius like Sofia to realize that Regan does not like this.

At all.

Regan can imagine how much more trouble she'll be in if Ms. Stein finds out that not only did they go through her bag (and what *is* all that stuff?), but they're reading her notebook.

(Let me assure you, an extra *month* of detention is nothing compared to what Ms. Stein has in store for them. And yes, that was blood. *Yuck.*)

"I don't really think . . ." Regan begins.

Sofia shoots her a look. "*We know.*"

Regan snaps her mouth shut. See, this is *exactly* why Regan's a little scared of Sofia. Regan doesn't need Sofia to remind her that she's not as smart as her.

But still . . . *rude.*

Darius looks down at the journal. "Maybe it can explain a few things."

The Journal of Victoria Francesca Stein is opened, and it's full of frantic scrawls, equations, and drawings of the human body.

It makes about as much sense to Regan as whenever she tries to do word jumbles. With her dyslexia, she has enough trouble seeing certain words when they're in the correct order. When words are purposely scrambled, it hurts her head.

But she's not the only one struggling with these drawings and scribbles.

"I don't understand. What does it mean?" Darius asks.

"Give it here." Sofia grabs the journal and starts flipping through the pages. Her eyebrows are furrowed as she scans Ms. Stein's writings. "This makes no sense. There's no possible way Ms. Stein wants to . . ."

Regan doesn't know Sofia that well, but she usually is annoyed (as we know all too well at this point—and we're only in chapter seven!). But right now, Sofia looks confused. And disturbed.

That can't be good.

Sofia sits down at a desk. "This has to be a joke."

"What does it say?" Bennett takes the journal back and starts reading from it. "'*I will be applauded for my work. For years, teachers have struggled with their students. Children today don't want to work. They have no patience, and they're difficult. But I know how to make the perfect student.*'" Bennett looks up. "Perfect student? How?"

Sofia grabs the journal back and opens it up on the desk to show a drawing of the human body. "She wants to replicate the best parts of a person and, ah . . ."

"What do you mean 'best parts'?" Darius takes a big gulp, the color beginning to pale on his dark brown skin. He glances at the needle and bloodied bag.

"She wants my smarts, Regan's kindness, Darius's loyalty, and Bennett's likability."

"Can't blame her for that," Bennett says as he pops the collar on his jacket.

"Are you serious right now?" Darius exclaims in a loud voice.

"Shh!" Sofia scolds him.

"But *how* is she going to replicate that?" Darius asks in a whisper.

A thought comes to Regan. She thinks about the detective shows her parents watch in the evening. Her hand goes back to the tender part of her head. "DNA," she says mostly to herself.

"What?" Bennett asks.

All three students turn and focus on Regan. Suddenly she feels foolish. When she's home, she has no trouble taking command of her siblings or giving house tours to the B&B's guests, but at school she doesn't feel as comfortable speaking up, *especially* in front of Sofia (and as we saw just a few pages ago, we know why). It's mostly because she's afraid to say the wrong thing. Like now. DNA? Really? What was she thinking? That's silly.

"She's right," Sofia says.

"I am?" Regan can hardly believe it. *And* that Sofia Vargas would admit it.

So not so silly after all. In fact, it's the opposite of silly, it's . . . about to get scary.

Sofia continues, "If I understand Ms. Stein's writing correctly— which I believe I do—she wants to collect our DNA and create creatures in our image that she can control."

"Wait a second!" Bennett turns to Sofia and points at her accusingly. "I told you!"

"Told her what?" Darius asks.

"Fine, fine." Sofia waves Bennett off.

"Oh, no. No, no, no." Bennett takes the notebook from Sofia. "You didn't believe me when I said that I saw a . . . a . . . *clone* of me yesterday."

"A clone?" Darius squeaks out. "And you're just mentioning this now?"

"Yes, well . . ." Sofia holds her hand out for the notebook.

Bennett clutches it close to him. "I think you owe me an apology, Sof."

"It's Sofia."

"*Sofia*, you have to admit that I was right for once! *I was right!*" Then Bennett's mouth falls open in shock. "Oh no, I was right."

Sofia simply holds her hand out in reply.

"Wait." Darius shakes his head. "I'm just . . . There's a *clone* of Bennett? I mean, how is that even possible?" He turns to Regan. "You said DNA?"

Regan's knee starts shaking. She's uncomfortable to have everybody waiting for her to speak.

She looks to Sofia, hoping maybe she'll talk instead, but Sofia gives Regan a nod, which for Sofia is a pretty big gesture.

Regan tries to stand a little taller. "So yeah, my household is a little chaotic. I've got four siblings: Roman, Rylee, River, and Rose, so there's a lot going on in the evenings. That's on top of seeing to the guests we have staying with us. But there are times in the evening when the rest of the kids are asleep—"

"Can you please skip to the ending?" Sofia asks with a scowl.

Again, *rude*. Although Sofia has a point. Ms. Stein could come back any minute.

Regan clears her throat. "Yeah, so DNA. That's how she's going to replicate us. She already has her samples. She took my hair yesterday, Bennett's saliva, and Sofia's and Darius's, ah, um . . ."

"Snot," Darius finishes for her.

Sofia grabs the notebook back from Bennett. "Yes, she took our DNA and . . ."

Remember before when I said that things get gross and scary? Well, buckle up or close your eyes, because we're about to go there. Although . . . how can you read if you close your eyes? Never mind that part, just grab your favorite stuffed animal so we can move on.

Ready?

Are you sure?

Okay. Let's do this.

"Ms. Stein collected our DNA in hopes to multiply it. Then by harnessing massive amounts of electricity, she'd be able to bring an obedient clone to life. She thinks she can create the perfect student. And if she makes enough of them, she'd basically have a clone army to take over the whole school."

I mean, that does sound pretty cool, huh? And maybe a little scary?

How is that scary?

Well . . .

Darius starts pacing the small room. "But if she creates clones of us—a whole army of so-called perfect students—what happens to us?"

"I don't think her plan includes us sticking around," Sofia says, her voice oddly steady. "We're her guinea pigs in creating a perfect student. If she does that, we'll be irrelevant."

"Irrelevant?" Regan says in a whisper. She's not so sure she wants to know what that means.

A cackle of Ms. Stein's laughter ricochets from down the hallway.

"Okay, that's it. We need to get out of here before she comes back." Darius grabs the journal and shoves it in his backpack. "We have proof that she *wants to clone us*. That she wants to take over the school with clones. But do you think it's going to stop there? If I've learned anything from reading comic books, it's that the endgame is always world domination. So yeah, we need to go to our parents and tell them what's going on. But first we need to get out of here *now*."

"But we'll get in trouble," Regan says.

Even Regan realizes *this* shouldn't be her concern right now, what with the threat of being cloned and then . . . But come on, there's no way that Ms. Stein—their teacher—would do this. That's ridiculous.

But then again, tell that to the back of Regan's head. And the bag of blood on the desk. And that giant needle.

The click-clack of Ms. Stein's shoes softly echoes down the hallway.

"She's coming!" Bennett says in a low hiss.

Click-clack.

Everybody turns to Sofia.

Click-clack.

"If we don't leave now, we'll be in even more trouble," Sofia says as she glances at the door.

Click-clack.

All of a sudden, the power goes out in the building.

"Mmmmmmhaaww," Ms. Stein cackles. "I hope you're ready, children."

Click-clack.

"Go now! *Now!*" The panic in Sofia's voice snaps everybody out of their confused daze.

The four take off down the hallway, not daring to look back to see how close Ms. Stein is. They're too busy running for their lives.

Literally.

8

Let me tell you something else you don't know about these four kids: They can run fast. Like, really, *really* fast.

But I guess running for your life from a mad science teacher and all that would help anybody pick up the pace.

They speed through the baseball field and arrive at the edge of the school grounds.

"Stop!" Darius calls out as he doubles over and grabs his side. "Where are we even running to?"

"Hey," Bennett says to Regan with a nod of respect. "You're surprisingly fast. Not bad."

Regan clenches her jaw. She wants to tell him that fat people can run and be active, but she's a little too distracted with the teeny-tiny fact that their science teacher *wants to clone them*.

"We should stick together," Darius suggests. "I think we have a better chance to be believed if we're a united front. Plus, there's only one notebook."

"I concur," Sofia . . . concurs. "We should go to my house—"

"*Our* house, future sis," Bennett corrects Sofia.

"*My* dad will be home soon and we can tell him," she replies with a scowl.

"Yeah!" Bennett nods along. "Sofia's dad is the coolest and he'll totally believe us and help us because he's, like, the greatest guy." Bennett beams at an—get ready to be shocked—annoyed Sofia.

(Okay, from now on, when I say anything about Sofia, you should just assume that she's annoyed. It's like her factory setting.)

But before I go on, you should also know something about Sofia's dad and Bennett. They are close, like super close. Maybe it's because Bennett's own father left him and his mom when he was six, so he likes having another dude around. It could also be that since Sofia's dad and Bennett's mom started dating—then got engaged, and eventually moved the families in together—Bennett has never seen his mom so happy. Because Diego Vargas is, in fact, a pretty awesome dude. He tosses the ball around with Bennett most nights after dinner, and he makes some delicious grub like tacos carnitas.

Do you want to know how Sofia seems to react to this?

Yep. It begins with *an* and ends with *noyed*.

The four begin the quick walk to Sofia and Bennett's old Victorian house only a few blocks away from school.

"Do you think Ms. Stein is following us?" Darius asks, looking over his shoulder for about the gazillionth (give or take a zillionth) time since they left detention.

Regan starts wringing her hands, that uneasy feeling back in her stomach.

"Are you okay, Regan?" Darius asks.

"It's just Ms. Stein is going to be so angry with us when she realizes we aren't in detention. *And* that we took her notebook."

Oh, I can assure you Ms. Stein is currently furious. As in steam-would-come-out-of-her-head-if-it-could mad. As in these-children-are-in-way-more-trouble-than-they-can-imagine-and-Ms.-Stein-wants-revenge mad.

"True," Darius admits. "But I'd rather be here right now than back in detention. Who knows what she was going to do next?"

Regan balls up her skirt in her hands. "But we still have school tomorrow. It's not like we can avoid Ms. Stein forever." Just the thought of stepping into Ms. Stein's classroom or detention again makes the strawberry yogurt Regan had as an after-school snack creep its way up her throat. "What are we supposed to do about tomorrow?"

Sofia stops in her tracks. "We have bigger issues to deal with than class tomorrow." She whips around to face Bennett. "And don't you dare tell me to *just relax*."

Bennett throws his hands up in the air. "Are you kidding me? We should be doing the opposite of relaxing! Or worrying about school! Ms. Stein has a clone of me, and she wants to"—he takes a big gulp—"get rid of us. This is no time to relax!"

So ah, remember when I said Bennett was a cool guy who didn't let things bother him?

Never mind!

Sofia nods with a satisfied smile on her face. "For once we agree on something. Now, let's get to it." Sofia leads the way, speed walking the next two blocks until the crew finds themselves on the front porch of her house.

"Oh good, they're both home," Bennett says as he points to the two cars in the driveway.

Sofia pauses before opening the door. "Let me do all the talking. We need to focus on facts and proof." She holds up Ms. Stein's notebook. "And don't get hysterical." She shoots Bennett a not-so-subtle glare.

The four detention-mates enter the Norland-Vargas household. The front living room is light and airy, filled with bright furniture and decorated with pictures from both families—together and separate.

"Dad?" Sofia calls out.

"In the kitchen, Sof!" a voice calls out from down the hallway.

Instead of correcting her father with an *it's Sofia* like she does with Bennett, Sofia dashes down the hallway. The rest follow behind her.

At the kitchen table sits Sofia's father. He and Sofia share the same big brown eyes, upturned nose, and wavy dark hair. He lights up as they enter the room. His smile is almost as bright as the orange-and-yellow pumpkin tie he's wearing, which is very different from his daughter's uniform of a black T-shirt and jeans, which Sofia wears every day. (I'll get into *that* later.)

"Sof! B-man! You've brought some friends!" Mr. Vargas says as he stands up to greet the crew.

"Dad, we have—" Sofia begins, but her dad pulls her into a hug.

"Now, now, let's have introductions. So nice to have you in our home. I'm Diego, proud father of this one!" He gives Sofia a big squeeze. "And soon to be the old man to this fine fellow over there." He gives Bennett a wink, at which Bennett can't help but beam back at Diego.

"Hello, Mr. Vargas, I'm Regan," Regan says as she extends her hand. Running for their lives or not, she does know her manners.

"Diego, please," he replies as he gives Regan a warm shake. "And I know your parents quite well, Regan. How's business at the Bed and Boofast? I was just thinking of contacting your folks about a Halloween open house I want to do. I think it would be fun to have a decorating contest for all the tourists."

"Dad—" Sofia protests.

He then turns his attention to Darius. "And of course, I know Darius."

Darius blushes as he extends his hand. "Thanks for having us, sir," Darius replies, also raised with manners.

"Had I known we'd have Cauldron's Cove royalty in the house, I would've cleaned up," he says with a wink.

Oh, here's something you should know about Darius: His mother is the mayor of Cauldron's Cove. So everybody in town knows Darius. *Everybody*. He's often featured in the local newspaper with his family at events around town. Then there are all these boring fundraisers and campaign stops where he has to wear a stuffy suit and tie. He's usually the only kid, and his sixteen-year-old sister, Tiana, is always glued to her phone. So Darius gets stuck having to pose for pictures with random people, and sometimes he even gets his cheeks pinched. And yes, it's just as embarrassing as you'd think it is.

"When your mother told me you made those delicious cookies for the pet shelter this summer, I couldn't believe it." Sofia's dad pats his belly. "In fact, I think we should do a junior baking competition to highlight the talented youth of our community, although we already know who would win."

At this compliment, not having to do with his mother, Darius puffs his chest out in pride.

"Now, can I get any of you—"

"Dad!" Sofia snaps. "Nobody wants anything! We have something really big to talk to you about!"

(So much for keeping it calm, I see . . .)

"What's going on?" A pale white woman with a sandy brown bob enters the kitchen, wearing medical scrubs decorated with cartoon witches. "Oh, we have—"

"Melony, this is Regan and Darius from detention; Regan and Darius, this is Bennett's mom," Sofia says in record time. "Can we please tell you what's going on before it's too late?"

"My goodness, this sounds serious," Bennett's mom says as she sits down next to Sofia's dad. They exchange a worried look at Sofia's ominous tone, but then . . .

WARNING: A disgusting, gag-inflicting form of adult affection is about to take place!

"Hello, my love, how was your day?" Sofia's dad says as he plants a kiss on Bennett's mom's lips.

Ewwww. Give me weird goo and cloning over *that* any day.

Sofia lets out a groan. "I have something to tell you!"

"Sorry. Of course, sweetheart," Bennett's mom says with a smile that fades when she looks at the four kids in front of her. "You all do look a little . . . unsettled."

"Yes." Sofia takes a deep breath. "There is something we feel you should know about Ms. Stein."

And then Sofia tells them everything. About the ridiculous reasons they were each put in detention. About the hair, snot, and spit. About the notebook. About the clones. About the plan.

To their credit, the two adults sit quietly and wait for Sofia to finish.

". . . and that's why we left detention to come straight here."

The kitchen is so quiet you can only hear the refrigerator buzzing in the corner. All four kids wait in anticipation for what the grown-ups are going to say. What plan they'll come up with to help them.

Mr. Vargas (because I was also raised to respect my elders, *thank-youverymuch*) nods a bit before looking at Ms. Norland. They lock eyes for a moment before they both start laughing. The oh-my-goodness-that-is-the-funniest-thing-I-ever-heard kind of laugh. The kids-are-so-hilarious-I-can't-believe-they-thought-we'd-fall-for-that laughter. And it goes on.

And on.

And on.

Finally, Mr. Vargas wipes away a tear from his eye. "You got me, mija. For a second I thought you were serious with the notebook, and then—" He slaps the table as he collapses into another fit of giggles.

Okay, *who* exactly are the adults here?

"Oh, Sofia, sweetie, did Bennett put you up to this?" Ms. Norland shakes her head at her son. "Here I was hoping Sofia would be a better influence on you!"

"No, it's fine!" Mr. Vargas says. "When I was your age, I got caught up in the ghosts-and-witches-and-things-that-go-bump-in-the-night spirit of our fair city. There was one Halloween I was even too scared to go outside after a particularly convincing witches' coven performance in the town square. I get what you kids are going through."

"We aren't—" Sofia begins.

But Mr. Vargas lights up. "You know, you kids may have helped me! I've been thinking of different events to do in the spring. Maybe we should do a clone festival? Yes! We can get twins to come into town and compete in some kind of contest."

"Oh, that's a wonderful idea!" Ms. Norland nods along.

"Mom." Bennett finally speaks. "This isn't some idea for tourists. Sofia is telling you the truth! I saw a clone of myself yesterday."

Ms. Norland's mouth turns into a firm line. "Now, Bennett, that's enough. This little joke—"

"It's not a joke!" Bennett protests. "This is real!"

Sofia, Regan, and Darius all nod in agreement behind him.

Ms. Norland sighs. "Do you seriously expect me to think Vicky could do something like this?"

Oh yeah, here's something you should probably know: Vicky—aka Ms. Stein—is friends with Bennett's mom. They're in book club together. She's even been over to their house a few times.

"But she *did* do this!" Bennett says, his voice getting high. "You have to believe us!"

He gestures at Darius and Regan behind him.

"Yeah, it's, ah, true, ma'am," Darius says in such a soft voice he could hardly be heard.

Regan decides to take a step back, not wanting to get the wrath of another set of parents.

Ms. Norland stands up. "Look, I'm sure there's some perfectly reasonable explanation for this." She picks up her phone and puts it on speaker.

"What are you—" Sofia begins to protest but closes her mouth as soon as she hears Ms. Stein's voice fill the kitchen.

"Hello? Melony, is that you? Have you seen Bennett?" Ms. Stein's voice is unsteady, and her breath sounds winded.

To her credit, a look of concern does flash on Ms. Norland's face.

"Are you all right, Vicky? Bennett is here with Sofia, Regan, and Mayor Washington's son."

Regan couldn't help but notice that Darius cringed when being referred to only as the mayor's son. She gets it. She's seen as her siblings' sister or her parents' helper. Sometimes it would be nice to be just known for being you.

"They're supposed to be in detention!" Ms. Stein says, and you don't need to see her face to know that she is sneering and probably spitting, she's so mad.

Ms. Norland also looks upset. "I know, and believe me, Bennett and Sofia will answer for that. It's just . . . Vicky, and I'm so sorry to even bring this up to you, but they have this notebook, and they are—"

"They *stole* my notebook," Ms. Stein clarifies. "Before leaving detention without my permission."

Regan sinks against the kitchen wall. They are in *so* much trouble.

"Is that so?" Ms. Norland says as she holds up the notebook. "They didn't mention that."

"This wasn't how you were raised, Sofia," Mr. Vargas says with a disappointed nod. "You need to apologize to Ms. Stein. All of you need to, and I can't imagine that your mother will be happy to hear this, Darius."

Darius joins Regan against the wall. Being the son of the mayor puts more pressure on Darius than an average ten-year-old. He's not allowed to make mistakes like most of his friends. Everything he does is under a microscope.

Regan can't even look at Sofia and Bennett's parents right now. Maybe she does deserve to be in detention. She stole from a teacher. She skipped out of detention.

They all did.

Regan is starting to feel like maybe she's the true villain here.

"Ms. Stein is trying to clone us, Dad!" Sofia says as she throws her hands up in frustration.

Oh right, *that*.

"I would think taking her notebook for proof and running before she harmed us would be okay, given her plan!" Sofia exclaims.

There's laughter coming from the phone. "Oh, Sofia, I can't believe you read my ramblings and actually thought I was going to . . ."

More uncontrollable laughter from a so-called adult.

"I saw my clone!" Bennett exclaims, his voice near hysterics.

Jeez, it does seem like Bennett should maybe *just relax*.

"Clone?" Ms. Stein says. "Oh goodness, such an imagination you have, Bennett. You see, that notebook is just some ideas I've been brainstorming for a novel I've been thinking about writing."

(Okay, I have to admit that this all does seem like a truly genius idea for a book. Get ready to hand all the awards over to Ms. Stein if she gets this written: the Pulitzer, the Nobel Peace Prize, an unlimited lifetime supply of cheese fries . . .)

Ms. Stein continues, "Melony, you know how we discuss in book group what the author must be thinking when they're writing a story. As you can see from my incomprehensible ramblings, I've got the questionable mental state of an author down."

(Hey! I take offense!)

Ms. Norland gives a little laugh as she shakes her head in a kids-what-are-you-going-to-do way.

Can you believe that the parents are buying into Ms. Stein's lies? It's almost as if the adults are conspiring against kids! Maybe they're all in on it!

"I am so sorry, Vicky," Ms. Norland says as she looks at the four-some with a frown.

"They need to return to school immediately. I have a schedule to keep! We have much to do."

"They will be right there—" Ms. Norland begins.

"Ms. Stein," Sofia interrupts. "We are very sorry. We have already wasted enough of your time today. We will stay as long as you need tomorrow and can even come on Friday if you need."

Wait. What?

Regan's eyes fill with panic. Darius's mouth is hung open. Bennett is just blinking in disbelief.

What on earth is Sofia up to?

There's a pause on the line. "Well, yes, I may need some more time with you, so that would be acceptable."

"Well, I'm glad we've come to an agreement," Ms. Noland says with a sigh. "And Vicky, I'll be speaking to both Darius's and Regan's parents. I think I speak for all of us when I say that we'll respect whatever punishment you deem worthy for their behavior today."

"But, Mom—" Bennett begins, but she gives him such a withering stare, a chill goes down his spine.

"Thank you," Ms. Stein says. "I know exactly how they can make it up to me." Then Ms. Stein lets out a little cackle.

Uh-oh.

"And, children," Ms. Stein continues, "I so look forward to seeing you all at school tomorrow."

A teacher looking forward to seeing students at school?

Yeah, that's a threat.

9

Let's make sure we're all caught up on what's going on, because even *my* head is spinning. Ms. Stein is cloning or has already cloned the group to make some kind of army of perfect students to take over Cauldron's Cove. *Cool.* When the clones are completed, Ms. Stein won't need Sofia, Bennett, Regan, or Darius around. *Cool.* And even though they have proof, nobody will believe them. *Cool. Cool. Cool.*

"What on earth are we going to do?" Regan exclaims when the four leave the Norland-Vargas house.

"And why on earth did you tell Ms. Stein we'd spend extra days in detention, Sof?" Bennett asks.

"It's Sofia, and we need time to come up with a plan." Sofia paces around the front porch, a frown on her face, her hands wrapped up in tight fists.

Now, I know I said that Sofia is usually in a grumpy mood, but I'm sort of on her side on this one. Her father and future stepmother don't believe *her*. *Sofia!* The girl who does extra homework. Who reads big, thick books on history for *fun*.

And let's not forget the biggest worry of all: Sofia, Bennett, Regan, and Darius are going to have to go to school tomorrow.

They're going to have to face Ms. Stein.

Gulp.

"Okay, Regan and Darius, what about your parents?" Bennett asks. "We just need *one* adult to believe us."

Regan shakes her head furiously. "I-I-I'm sorry, but I can't. I'm already in too much trouble."

"No kidding," Darius replies. "Here I already thought it couldn't get worse, and now this." He gestures at the front door to the house, where Ms. Norland is no doubt calling his mother.

"But this is serious," Sofia states.

Regan's bottom lip starts to quiver. Regan can handle a lot, and she does, but this is just too much. She doesn't want to let the group down, *but* . . . "The last thing I want to do is cause any more work for my parents. You guys don't understand. There are five of us. I'm supposed to be the easy one. The helper. Not the one trying to convince them that my teacher . . ."

She couldn't even say it. There's no way a teacher could be that sinister, right?

(Oh, there is. In fact, if I were you, I'd think twice before turning your back on your science teacher. Who knows what they are up to?)

"Darius?" Bennett asks, a desperate tone in his voice. "Your mom is the mayor. Shouldn't she be aware that something like this is happening in her town? She has the power to stop it!"

Darius grimaces. "There is no way she's going to believe me. At dinner, she's always telling us about all the weird calls City Hall gets about people claiming to be witches or seeing ghosts."

"But you're her son," Bennett reasons.

Darius's shoulders slump. "Yes, I'm her son who reads a lot of comic books about zombies and demons. Okay, so like one time—and I mean *one* time—I thought there was a zombie in my closet and I may have interrupted an important phone call because I came into her home office screaming, and yeah, I maybe also grabbed my sister's field hockey stick on my way and gave Mom a scare. It ended up just being an old Halloween costume and not a zombie. So nobody in my family has let me live that down. Besides, she has a reelection coming up and doesn't need her son causing problems. I can already picture the headline: 'Mayor's Unhinged Son Accuses Teacher of Cloning.'"

"But it's true!" Bennett cries.

Sofia suddenly stops pacing and stands in front of Darius. "Wait a moment. Darius, you read a lot about fictional creatures like monsters, right?"

"Ah, yeah?" Darius replies. "I mean, I also like superheroes and stuff—"

"Yes, as I said, fictional, as there is no such thing as superheroes."

Sofia says that, but let me tell you, dear reader, what these kids are about to do is quite super and heroic. So what does that make them?

Exactly.

Sofia studies Darius. "I only read nonfiction, as I'm concerned with facts. I already find fiction to be a bit much, and that's on top of all these stories floating around Cauldron's Cove and the tourist traps. However, what we are dealing with *is* quite fantastical." Sofia grimaces, almost like she hates to admit that there is something otherworldly at play. "So with your expertise in these creatures, what could be the cause of something like this?"

Darius stares blankly at Sofia.

She continues, "What I mean is, if this were one of your comic books, what would be a likely explanation for *why* this is happening with Ms. Stein?"

"Oh." Darius lights up. "Oh! Yeah! Like she would need some sort of villain origin story. All the good ones have them. There's usually some event that happens that makes them evil, like a chemical spill or explosion at a science lab."

Darius nods thoughtfully for a moment; he even strokes his chin. Then his eyes get wide. "Wait a second. If you think about it, this all happened *after* the storm, which was pretty intense."

"And not expected," Sofia adds. "It wasn't in the forecast and came out of nowhere, and even the meteorologists were confused." Sofia nods in approval. "Go on."

"Oh!" Darius exclaims. Perhaps all those years spent reading comic books are going to help make sense of what's happening. "Maybe Ms. Stein got hit with lightning or something. Or like, maybe she was cursed and—"

Sofia takes a step back. "A curse?"

"Ah, yeah, like when—"

"I know what a curse is," Sofia snaps. She begins to pace back and forth so quickly, the other three can't help but just stare at her.

Back and forth.

Back and forth.

Back and forth.

(Anybody else getting dizzy?)

"What are you thinking, Sof?" Bennett asks.

"It's Sofia." She stops in her tracks. "I'm thinking about curses."

"Curses?" Regan says so quietly. She was already intimidated by Sofia, and now she's talking about curses. There goes that knotty feeling in her stomach. Will she ever feel normal again? No way can she handle a curse.

(Between you and me, reader, Regan can handle way more than she knows. Just you wait.)

"Do you remember when Ms. Seidenfeld told us to read a Halloween-themed book last fall for our English assignment?" Sofia throws out to the group.

Darius perks up. "Yeah, it was awesome. Anything spooky counted: Ghosts, zombies, monsters. I got to read *The Last Kids on Earth* for class. How cool is that?"

"Yes, well, as I mentioned, I don't really like fiction." Sofia wrinkles her nose in disgust. "So I read a nonfiction book from the late 1800s that I found in the archive section in the library. It was on Cauldron's Cove's real history with witches. The town likes to celebrate its name and play up that witches *allegedly* lived here, only with cartoons and in a family-friendly way. But the thing is, Cauldron's Cove does have a dark history. Not that I believe in witches or ghosts or zombies or any of that nonsense." Sofia rolls her eyes.

Okay, reader, I can tell you that Sofia may not believe right now, but she soon will. That kind of happens when you come *face-to-face* with spooky creatures.

"*However . . .*"

And here we go . . .

"I read this account about a witch named Ann Wilder who cursed Cauldron's Cove when she was burned alive at the stake."

"What?" Regan says, all color drained from her already pale cheeks. "But there's no . . ."

"Mention of it at all? No, it probably wouldn't go down well with a scoop of Frozen Potion at Black Cat Creamery. Or make a good background for tourist photos taken at Hocus Focus. People seem to forget how actually awful the Salem witch trials were. Even though it was over three hundred years ago, this town doesn't seem to want to come to terms with what it did."

"Wait." Regan scrunches up her face. "Didn't Ms. Stein mention something about having to wait three hundred years?"

"Yes, she did. So if Ann Wilder was indeed a witch, it could explain a curse. If there is one."

"Whoa," Darius replies. "Sometimes I think this town can be so fake—please don't tell anybody I said that with my mom and all. But honestly, I didn't think anything cool—or *real*—ever happened in Cauldron's Cove."

"How is any of this cool?" Bennett exclaims, while Regan leans against the porch railing for support. "You wouldn't think it was cool if there was a clone of you out there, Darius!"

Bennett then does something very unlike him. He actually runs his fingers through his meticulously styled hair, causing pieces to stand up in all different directions. But dang it all if it doesn't still look perfect. That kid really has it good.

"Just relax," Sofia says with a delighted snicker. "Besides, there's definitely a clone of Darius out there."

"What?" Darius cries out, panic finally creeping into his voice.

"Of course there is," Sofia replies, like this information is obvious and not a big deal. "If there's a clone of Bennett, there has to be clones of Darius, and Regan, and me. If you recall, Ms. Stein got samples from all of us."

Regan's eyes go wide as she touches the back of her head. But do you want to know a secret? (Of course you do!) For just a split second, like the teeny-tiniest amount of time that can actually be recorded, which, fun fact, is called a zeptosecond (oh wait, I promised no more learning! I'm so incredibly sorry! Here's a joke to make up for it: What's stinky and round and behind you? Your butt! Hey, I didn't say it was going to be a *good* joke) . . .

Where were we? Oh right, for a zeptosecond, Regan thought how nice it would be to have another one of her to split up all her chores. She'd totally have her clone change Rose's poopy diapers and clear the dining table, especially since both River and Rose drop more food than actually goes in their mouths. She'd have more time to do something she wanted. Because here's another secret about Regan: She loves to sing. She sings to her siblings and in the shower. While making beds at the B&B, she daydreams about being center stage, singing her heart out. She didn't have the confidence to try out for the choir at school, where Maisy Menzel always gets all the solos anyway. What if she got laughed at? Plus, it really didn't matter since she'd never be able to get the time off from all her sisterly duties to be in the school musicals.

Yeah, so Regan would love to have another one of her. And maybe, just maybe, her clone wouldn't have dyslexia and could do her homework.

But no, Regan shouldn't want any of that, since clones are bad.

Right?

"So what are we going to do?" Darius asks the all-important question that we all want answered.

Sofia starts walking away from the house. She pauses as she looks over her shoulder. "Well, come on, then, we need to get some answers."

10

Where have our heroes gone to get the help they need? When you think about it, there's only one place that can answer *almost* every question you may have. There are some that just can never be answered, like "What's the meaning of life?" "Why is my sibling so annoying?" "Is the narrator of this story playing with a full deck of cards?"

But as for Ann Wilder and the Cauldron's Cove curse (say *that* three times fast!), there's only one place Sofia knows will help.

"The library?" Bennett says as they stand before the Cauldron's Cove Public Library, which has a sign out front with their opening times, labeled as WITCHING HOURS.

This town and their puns.

"Yes, Bennett," Sofia says with a shake of her head. "I'm aware you may not be familiar, as it's not a soccer field or basketball court. It's a building that you can go into and get as many books as you want. Hm, I guess magic does exist."

"I know what a—" Bennett takes a deep breath. "What are we doing here?"

"We're here for research," Regan answers for Sofia. It seems pretty obvious to Regan. They need to find out more about Ann Wilder and the curse. Of course they'd go to the library. It sits in an old historic building near the town square. The basement even has a bunch of items from the town's long history.

"Exactly! Come along!" Sofia says as the rest, once again, fall in line behind her. "While I've been to the downstairs museum a bunch, I'll give one more look to see if there's any mention of Ann Wilder. Then I will find the original text I used for my book report. Bennett and Regan, you go online and see what you can find. Darius, I want you to read everything you can about the storm the other day."

"So we could've totally done this at home on the internet?" Bennett complains.

Sofia narrows her eyes at him. "No, I need the historic book made with actual pages. It's where I first read about the curse. Then we need to cross-verify with periodicals and other paper resources. And then—"

"Okay, okay!" Bennett throws his hands up as they enter the library.

Sofia marches to the back, while the rest settle down at the computer hub.

Darius sets his backpack on a chair. "I think I'm going to look at the newspapers from the day after the storm." He goes over to the front desk.

Leaving Bennett and Regan alone.

"So, ah, I guess I'll just see what I can find on Ann Wilder," Regan says, even though she feels a little foolish. What exactly would they find? Did this supposed witch really curse the town, and why would it take this long for something to finally happen? And even if it's true, why Ms. Stein? Why Regan? Why any of them?

"Yo, B-ball!" Stu Ripley calls out to Bennett from across the library, getting not-even-subtle glares from the rest of the patrons trying to soak in the peaceful glory that is the public library. "What up?"

"Yo, man!" Bennett replies as they do some complicated dude-bro slap thing that they probably spent days perfecting. Not that they would ever admit to such a thing. "Sup?"

Boys and their conversations, am I right?

Regan starts typing away and finds a bunch of blogs about the Salem witch trials. And drawings of witches. Being hanged. And set on fire.

Nope, her stomach does not like this at all. It keeps twisting and turning as she sees headlines like "Cast Out All Witches and Devils" and "Conference Concerning Evil Spirits." Plus, Regan needs to concentrate when she's reading, and it's really hard for her right now because—

"What are you doing here, bro? I thought you had detention?" Stu says, as he plunks down next to Regan, smashing his backpack into her arm.

"Ah, yeah, um." Bennett sneaks a glance around the library. "We're here to do some research for detention."

"So not fair, dude."

"Yeah, dude."

Dude, Regan really needs to focus and—

"You missed a killer practice. Coach had us do sprints, but then we got to spend the rest of the practice tackling. It was dope."

"Dope."

You know what *isn't* dope? Having dudes duding when Regan wants to get to the bottom of what's going on. But she doesn't want to draw Stu's attention, since he can be a bit of a bully. You should probably know that Stu is large like Regan. However, he uses his size to smash into people during football, so he's praised for his size, not criticized, which really isn't fair. We all come in different shapes and sizes. How boring would it be if we all looked like Bennett?

Let's face it, Bennett would probably think that would be the greatest thing . . . at first. But then Bennett wouldn't be special because everybody looked like him. *Boring*.

Anyhoo, Stu leans back and his chair pinches Regan's arm. She scooches over to get some space. Regan takes a deep breath, something she does when her siblings are testing her patience, which is basically all the time.

Instead of reading, since it's hard with all the *dudes* and *bros* being hurled in front of her, she decides to focus on images. Besides, she's a better visual learner. Maybe there'll be a picture or graph or—

Wait a second, what's *that*?

Regan finds an old map of Cauldron's Cove from when Ann Wilder was alive. You know, the times before flushing toilets and the internet—*gasp*! Back then, the town was much smaller, with only a few houses near the river. She zooms in to find Ann's house, the one the town set on fire before burning her.

"Ah, Bennett," Regan says, wanting someone to confirm what she's seeing.

"Oh, didn't see you there, Regan the Rhino," Stu says with a snort. "Which is odd since you're hard to miss." Stu then puffs out his cheeks.

Regan ignores him. She has more important things to worry about than a bully. Plus, if someone has to be mean to her to feel better about themselves, that is sad as far as Regan is concerned.

"B-ball, don't tell me you're here with Rhino?" Stu asks Bennett.

"Oh, well, ah . . ." Bennett's pale cheeks turn red. He glances at

Regan for a second before looking back at his computer screen. "I mean, we were in detention together, but it's not like we're—"

Ouch.

Okay, here's something else you should know about Regan. She can handle a lot. Being a second mother to her siblings. Waking up early on the weekends to clean the guest rooms and do laundry for the B&B. Having to work twice as hard only to get averages grades. Being teased for her weight. But *this*, Bennett not wanting to admit he's here with Regan—that's just cruel. Okay, yes, it's not like the four of them are friends. They just all happened to be put in detention and are on this bizarre journey together.

But truth be told, Regan wishes she had more friends. She's too busy for extracurriculars. Nobody in school wants to be paired with her for class assignments, since it takes her longer to do the work. She sits at lunch with Zoey Ito, since they're both in special needs classes for their learning differences, but besides that they don't have a ton in common.

Regan's constantly surrounded by people—her family, guests, classmates—but sometimes she feels really alone.

Even now, being with the three other students and in the middle of the library, Regan feels lonely.

Stu snorts. "Yeah, I figured you wouldn't want to hang out with—"

"I've got it!" Sofia cuts off Stu. She's carrying a thick, old book with a red leather cover and yellow pages.

"Hey!" Darius comes running over. "You're not going to believe what I found." He plops down a newspaper with a map of the storm from the other night.

"Dude, are you, like, working with these people?" Stu laughs like there's some joke only he knows the punch line for. "And here I thought being with the Rhino was bad enough."

Uh-oh. While Regan will remain quiet to not cause problems, there is one person who certainly doesn't have time for Stu. Someone who finds even kind and well-meaning people annoying.

Yup.

Sofia walks right up to Stu. Even with him sitting and her standing, he still towers over her. "We have important things to discuss, Stuart. It's best for you to be on your way."

"Are you seriously—"

Sofia leans in, only inches from his smug face. "Are *you* too thick in the head to not understand what I'm saying? Got tackled a few too many times to figure out when someone is telling you to get lost? Do you think it's okay to give people mean nicknames because of their size? Because I've got a few names I'd like to call you."

Regan looks down at the floor, trying to suppress a smile. She knows that Sofia is also being a bit of a bully, but she can't help but enjoy Stu getting a taste of his own medicine.

"Ah . . ." Stu says as Sofia starts poking him in the chest.

"You. Go. Now."

Stu looks over at Bennett, who shrugs. "Yeah, man, we've got some stuff to do with detention and all. I'll catch you later."

"Whatever, dude," Stu says as he walks away, narrowly missing Regan's face as he swings his backpack.

"I can't believe you're friends with someone like that," Sofia says with a shake of her head.

"I just—"

Sofia holds her hand up and turns to Regan. "I hope you're aware that no one should be judged by their size."

Regan can only give a small nod. She does know that. She really does, but that doesn't mean it doesn't sting when someone can't see beyond her weight.

But there's a softness to Sofia now. That fear Regan has of her is slowly melting away. Not entirely, because as it was just made clear, Sofia has no problem telling people off. But still, Regan appreciates Sofia for standing up for her.

"And you!" Sofia narrows her eyes at Bennett. "You should know that just because some might consider you to be debatably attractive by Western standards, that doesn't mean you're a good person. Or a good friend."

Ouch. But also *true*.

Bennett looks down at the floor, embarrassed. "Sof, I didn't—"

"It's Sofia." She slams the book down on the table with a thud. "We've got more important things to discuss."

Regan finds her shoulders relaxing slightly with the attention off her and back on Ann Wilder. And then right back up her shoulders go when she remembers they are dealing with a witch's curse.

Sofia continues, "First, the downstairs had no mention of Ann Wilder at all. None. It's like the town wants to forget about her. But this book, where I originally read about her, had something interesting. Ann Wilder was killed on September twenty-fourth."

"Wait, that was just a few days ago." Darius holds up the newspaper. "It was the date of the storm."

"The anniversary of her death. So we know *why* it's happening now."

"And this!" Darius points at the bright red blob on the newspaper. "This is a satellite image at the peak of the storm. It's concentrated on Maple Street. Where Ms. Stein lives. I totally knew the storm had something to do with whatever's going on."

Regan's eyes go wide as she looks between where Darius's finger is pointing and what's on her screen.

It can't be, can it?

"It would make sense that the curse and storm are related," Sofia says as she studies the image.

"Ah . . ." Regan starts, but her voice gives out.

"So the curse caused the storm on the anniversary of Ann Wilder's death. So maybe Ms. Stein got hit by lightning?"

"Yeah," Darius agrees. "Bennett mentioned lightning *inside* Ms. Stein's."

"Um, guys." Regan tries to get their attention, but she isn't being as loud as she needs to be. Because what if she's wrong? She doesn't want this group to regret being stuck with her.

"But what ties Ms. Stein with the curse?" Sofia asks aloud. "Why her?"

"I think I have something," Regan tries again, raising her voice.

Darius is too wrapped in his conversation with Sofia to hear Regan. "It's like this origin story I was telling you about—"

"CAN YOU PLEASE LISTEN TO ME!"

Every head in the library turns to the group and Regan covers her mouth. She can't believe she just yelled, but if she's right, this could be the break they need.

"Yes?" Sofia says with a raised eyebrow. "You certainly have our attention, Regan. Ours and everybody else's in the library. Did you find something?"

Regan turns the computer screen toward them. "I found this old map of Cauldron's Cove from Ann Wilder's time." Regan puts her finger near an *X* on the map, the exact location where Darius has his finger on his map. "This is where Ann Wilder's house was."

It's the exact same place where the storm was at its worst.

It's also where Ms. Stein lives.

"Whoa," Bennett replies.

"Now we know *why* Ms. Stein." Sofia nods in approval at Regan. "None of this can be brushed aside as coincidences. The only explanation is that Ann Wilder was indeed a witch and this curse is real."

Gulp.

11

For a moment, a teeny-tiny moment (a zeptosecond, if you will), Regan felt smart. She felt good about herself. She—the girl who gets snickered at in class when she mispronounces words during read-alouds or has to stay after to finish a math test—made the connection that could finally provide some answers!

But then Sofia had to come up with a crazy plan that makes Regan want to crawl into the children's reading nook and pretend the last two days never happened.

And she's not the only one who finds Sofia's idea . . . not the best.

"You want us to do *what*?!" Bennett exclaims as the group stands outside the library.

"Listen," Sofia says in a calm voice. "We have so many questions about what's happening and we need answers. We need to know *why* Ms. Stein is doing this."

"Ah, because she's cursed!" Bennett replies, his voice teetering on hysterics.

"Just relax," Sofia says with a smirk. "Yes, she's cursed. But we need to know what her plan is. Darius used the word 'endgame' about the villains he reads about. So what's Ms. Stein's endgame with the clones?"

"In the notebook she said she just wants students to behave better," Darius replies.

"Yes, but do you really think she's going to make a clone out of us and then be on her merry way? Ms. Stein made clones because she wants to replace us. Think about it: She picked us because she *likes* certain qualities we each have. We're the *good* students and we're still in trouble. What's going to happen to the so-called bad ones? What about people like your *bro* Stu?"

Bennett takes a step back as he realizes what Sofia's suggesting. "You mean, she wants to get rid of all the students and only have some clone army?"

"But . . ." Regan starts, then hesitates. She had one moment where she was helpful, and she doesn't want to ruin it by arguing with anyone, especially Sofia. But also . . . "I know your parents didn't believe us, but at some point *someone* has to. Parents aren't going to sit around and let their children be replaced. I'd like to think mine would notice if there was a clone of me instead of their actual daughter."

"But wait," Bennett says. "Maybe there's just the clone of me? You said she was going to take all the best parts of us and make the perfect student. It would make sense she'd use my body."

(Ugh, okay, there are some instances when Bennett is *not* likable. This is one of them.)

"We don't know, which is precisely why we have no other choice," Sofia says. "Whatever Ms. Stein is up to isn't good. And to be honest, I think it goes beyond the four of us. I think the whole town is in trouble. Ann Wilder cursed the children of Cauldron's Cove because she wanted the parents to suffer. But since no one will believe us, we need to be the ones to figure it out."

"We can't just—" Bennett begins, but then just shakes his head as if what Sofia has planned is the craziest thing that's happened so far.

While Regan only has one word going through her head: *Nope. Nope. Nope. Nope. Nope. NO-PE. No way. No way. Just no way.*

Okay, that's more than one word, but you get the idea.

It doesn't matter what Sofia says or how much trouble the town is in, Regan can't be part of Sofia's plan.

What *is* Sofia's plan, you might be asking?

Good point, I should probably get to that.

"How many times do I have to say this?" Sofia says slowly, like she's talking to a small toddler. "The answers to our questions are in Ms. Stein's house. That's where the lightning struck. That's where she's made the clones. There's a chance we can stop what's happening there." She turns to Bennett. "Tell me everything you remember seeing when you were at her house yesterday. Don't leave out a single detail."

"Ah . . ." Bennett freezes.

Here's something else you should know about Bennett: He doesn't really freeze. If a tough shot needs to be made right at the buzzer during a basketball game, you give Bennett the ball. And he's always quick with a quip or a reply.

However, his future stepsister has never asked *him* for help before. And by the way Bennett is shuffling nervously on his feet, it seems to be freaking him out.

I mean, let's face it, if *you* had Sofia glaring at you to give her information that could potentially save your town, you'd also feel a little under pressure.

Sofia presses, "You're the only one of us who knows what's inside the house. This information is extremely important, so you need to remember everything exactly as it was."

"Yeah, um . . ." Bennett takes a gulp.

"But please, take your time, Bennett. No rush at all. It's only the fate of Cauldron's Cove hanging in the balance."

"Okay!" Bennett cries out. "It's just I told you everything the second I got home yesterday when it was all fresh and stuff, and you didn't believe me, and, like, I don't remember every detail like you."

Sofia sniffs. "I've already acknowledged what happened yesterday."

(Now, reader, did you notice how Sofia didn't apologize? The words *I'm sorry* didn't pass her lips. Told you she was super smart and frustratingly smug.)

"But when you think about it," Sofia continues, "would *you* believe *me* if I came home and said something as ridiculous as the tale you spun yesterday?"

"Yes," Bennett replies without hesitation.

Sofia's face is scrunched up in confusion. "No, you wouldn't."

"*Yes, I would,*" Bennett replies firmly. "Like it or not, we're family. And family needs to be there for each other. Family trusts each other. Family has each other's back."

Regan nods along. She would do anything for her family.

But it isn't lost on Regan that her family would never believe her if she told them the truth about what was really going on. Sure, her siblings would. They're little and think Regan is best friends with Santa

Claus, which always comes in handy when they start misbehaving around Christmas.

But her parents? No way.

Bennett starts pacing, his face scrunched up in concentration. "Okay, so I saw this, like, big metal round thingy that had, like, lightning coming from it, and then there was this, like, greenish stuff in vials. And, um, also there were drawings and stuff all over." Bennett balls his fists up, as if he's almost frustrated that he can't give more details. He only saw the room for a few seconds before his clone popped up in front of him.

"That lightning or whatever has to be from the storm," Darius replies. "It must be how Ms. Stein harnessed enough energy to turn our snot and stuff into clones. Maybe that green goo is what she mixed our DNA with. So Sofia is right. Ms. Stein's lair *is* the best place to get answers."

"Lair?" Sofia asks.

"Ah, yeah, all the villains in comic books have a lair where they plot out their evil plans," he explains.

Regan's head is spinning. She was already in so much trouble, there's just no way she can even for a second think about doing what Sofia is suggesting, what Darius seems to be on board with.

Nope.

Nope.

Nope.

"Excellent," Sofia says with a wide smile.

Regan finally decides to try to reason with them. "You can't seriously expect us to *break into Ms. Stein's house*?"

"That's exactly what I'm planning," Sofia responds, as if she's talking about what she's going to pack for lunch tomorrow, not breaking and entering.

(Dear reader, my publisher has informed me that I must make it clear that under no circumstances should you break into your teacher's—or anybody's—house. I have hereby decreed it and have absolved myself, your lovable rogue of a narrator, and them from any future possible litigation from any break-ins caused by reading this book. Unless your teacher is trying to clone you, then go right ahead!)

Darius takes a step forward. "I am in."

"You can't be serious, Darius," Bennett says.

"Are you kidding me?" Darius replies as he throws his hands up. "We can be heroes! I can actually *do* something besides wave from a podium next to my mom. And if we pull this off, who isn't going to vote for the woman whose son helped save Cauldron's Cove? Maybe a comic book will be written about *us*."

"Why does it have to be us?" Regan says. "We're just kids."

"Speak for yourself," Sofia, the youngest of them, replies.

"But someone has to believe us," Regan argues, desperate for this not to be left up to the four of them. There has to be a better way.

As far as Regan sees it, she feels bad, but someone else needs to handle this. Preferably someone with a driver's license and a mortgage—whatever that is, she just hears her parents talk about it a lot. It seems stressful and very adult. Like one giant headache. And stomachache.

Besides, Regan can't add "save the town of Cauldron's Cove" to her already packed to-do list.

"*Who* is going to believe us, Regan?" Darius challenges her. "Nobody, so *we* need to be the heroes. There might not even be a town of Cauldron's Cove left for my mother to run if we don't do something. And if I've learned anything from my comic books, it's that every villain has their kryptonite. And we're only going to find Ms. Stein's weakness if we break into her house. So, yeah, I am totally in."

Darius holds out his hand into the middle of the group. Sofia looks at his lone hand in confusion.

"Ah, this is when you put your hand in," Darius explains. "I'm trying to have a powerful team moment here! Come on!"

"Oh," Sofia says, and for a second something flashes on her face that is *not* annoyance. Was Sofia embarrassed not to know such a simple act of being on a team as putting your hands in? Is it even possible for Sofia Vargas to be embarrassed?

Sofia puts her hand on top of Darius's. She looks at Bennett, who shuffles on his feet for a second.

He takes a deep breath. "I think this is a horrible idea and will probably end in disaster, but I'm not going to let you do this without me, sis."

"I am not—" Sofia starts, but then simply sighs.

Three hands in. They all look at Regan.

Every hero has a moment. When they must decide to risk everything—their safety, their schoolwork, their stuffed animal collection—to do the right thing. To fight for others. To be brave when what they really want to do is run away.

This is Regan's moment.

What will she do? Take the hard road or run away?

What would *you* do?

Yeah, I had a feeling you're just like Regan. Selfless. Brave. Awesome.

Regan puts her hand in the middle. "I'm in."

12

Confession time: I've been keeping something from you.

While it's not in my nature to hold back, sometimes for dramatic effect, it's best to keep a few secrets.

And I've been keeping *three*.

Remember when Sofia mentioned that if there was a Bennett clone, there surely had to be clones of the rest of them?

Of course you do! You're so smart and clever and I'm sure have slightly above-average hygiene.

Well, there are. Three more clones to be exact.

Are you now curious about what these clones could be up to?

It's not as if they'd just be hanging out at Ms. Stein's house. Because that would be really, really boring. Plus, what's the point of clones if not to cause havoc and mischief?

So after Ms. Stein talked to Sofia's mother, she let them loose.

Why?

Well, you're about to see . . .

Near Witches' Way in downtown Cauldron's Cove is a pretty little town square. Next to the orange-and-black gazebo that sits in the middle is a sign with all the upcoming Haunted Happenings in Cauldron's Cove: Friday Night Movie Fright, Potent Potions, Broom-Making Class, Haunted Cemetery Tour, and Zombie 5K. There is also a "Welcome to Cauldron's Cove" message from none other than Mayor Washington with a picture of her in a witch's costume, flanked by three zombies— her husband and children, Darius and Tiana.

The square is full of people enjoying a lovely late September day. Cauldron's Cove residents mix with tourists wearing kitschy witchy T-shirts with black cats or sayings like WITCH PLEASE or WE ARE THE DAUGHTERS OF THE WITCHES YOU COULDN'T BURN. They're drinking spiced tea and nibbling on eyeball pops and candy apples from the nearby Witches Brew and SandWitch Shop.

It is quite the picturesque scene. The kind the town likes to highlight on the website Sofia's dad runs for the Cauldron's Cove Visitors Center.

Are you curious as to *why* we are in this square?

You see, this is where we find Darius and Sofia. But wait a second, we just saw them coming up with a plan several blocks away. Nope, these are their clones.

Hold on, you may be thinking. *Didn't Ms. Stein say she needed more from the students? It seemed like she wasn't happy with the clones, right?*

You *are* right! Because while these clones resemble Sofia and Darius, they aren't complete. On the surface they look like their counterparts, but upon closer inspection the details aren't right. Just like with Clone Bennett, their features aren't defined. Clone Darius's skin is dull, and he walks with a slump in his shoulders. Real Sofia's light brown skin is tinted green on Clone Sofia. And the Sofia clone also has a permanent scowl. You may be thinking, *But doesn't Sofia usually have a scowl?* Well, yes, nothing gets by you! However, Clone Sofia's face is the kind you're warned about when you make a silly face and are told by a grown-up that "if you keep making that face, it'll freeze that way." Well, that's a bunch of hooey. Yes, I said hooey!

Although Clone Sofia's face *does* look like it had been frozen after a particularly mean scowl.

But that's not the thing that really separates the clones from the real people . . . or actual human beings in general. You see, dear reader, they smell. Really bad. Really, *really* bad. Like sulfur.

What does sulfur smell like? Well, like disgustingly rotten eggs.

Or a super stinky fart.

Think back to the worst fart you've ever smelt (or dealt): It's like two thousand times worse.

So yeah, these clones stink.

Unsuspecting picnic-goers' noses twitch as Clone Darius and Clone Sofia stroll by.

"Isn't that Mayor Washington's son?" a young woman asks her husband as they sit with their baby on a picnic blanket. The baby is playing with a rattle as the couple eat from a picnic lunch of sandwiches and fruit.

It really would be a shame to have such a nice family moment ruined.

"Darius!" she calls out.

Clone Darius turns and starts walking toward the couple. Clone Sofia follows. (That alone should tip everyone off to something suspicious happening. We all know the real Sofia prefers to do the leading.) The woman has a smile on her face until she realizes Clone Darius is glaring at her. He bends down to the cooing baby and snatches the rattle away, causing the baby to start wailing. Clone Darius shakes the rattle a few times, studying the red-and-yellow plastic. Then he tosses it aside.

"Hey!" the woman protests. "What do you think you're doing?"

Clone Darius replies by kicking the picnic basket over while Clone Sofia walks on top of the food.

Pretty rude, that Clone Darius and Clone Sofia.

"Stop it!" the father shouts out.

"Ahhhhh . . ." Clone Darius replies.

Oh, did I forget to mention that the clones have a very limited vocabulary?

"Darius!" the woman cries, but the two clones have already made their way over to another blanket, stomping and being general nuisances.

"If Mayor Washington can't control her son, she certainly doesn't have my vote!" the man says as he holds his crying baby.

"That's it! I'm calling the mayor's office," the woman replies as she picks up her phone.

Uh-oh.

You see what's happening here? When Real Darius gets home, his mother is going to be so mad at him for what he did. He'll deny it because Darius *didn't* do it. You know that. I know that. But nobody else knows that. His mother will think Darius is lying.

And then she'll never believe him when he tells her that his science teacher has cloned him.

That's why Ms. Stein unleashed the not-quite-ready clones on the town.

To discredit the real kids.

Yep, that Ms. Stein is pretty smart.

You definitely don't want to be on her bad side.

Too bad Darius, Sofia, Regan, and Bennett didn't know that back in chapter seven when they stole her notebook.

As Clone Sofia and Clone Darius cause chaos in the town square, we find Clone Regan walking down Witches' Way, aka downtown's main street.

Besides stinking up the sidewalk, Clone Regan walks with a large bounce, as if she were walking on a trampoline. But that isn't why people are staring at her. It's because this Regan is loud. She's singing "Lalalalaaaalaaalaaaa" in a low, off-key monotone voice as she bounces down the sidewalk.

It's almost as if she's trying to find her voice.

Huh, maybe Real Regan can learn from her clone?

There's pounding on a window as Clone Regan walks past. "Rey! Rey! Rey!" is called out by two tiny ginger kids. It's River and Rose, Regan's youngest siblings. They stare up at the clone from a large window at Cauldron's Cove Community Childcare: *Where We Watch Over Your Little Witches and Wizards*. Because even the day care center in town has to have a witchy slogan.

Clone Regan pauses and tilts her head, as if she's trying to figure out who these two small creatures are who are excited to see her.

The siblings wave. They make faces. They pick their noses. They pee in their diapers. They tap on the window.

Clone Regan walks up to the glass and puts her hand against it, hard enough to make the window rattle.

River and Rose laugh in delight and clap at their supposed sister being silly.

Clone Regan studies her hand again and thwacks it against the glass, causing the two siblings to jump back, startled at the force.

River's chin starts to quiver and Rose grabs his hand.

A day care employee approaches the window from inside. "Regan? Are you okay?" She studies Regan with furrowed brows. "You really shouldn't be so rough with—"

Just then Clone Regan hits the window even harder, causing everybody inside the day care to back away from the glass. River starts to cry, which then causes Rose to cry, and before you know it, practically every kid in the center is bawling.

See, while these clones are flawed, there was one thing Ms. Stein got right. She wanted her clones to have super strength. Which they do. They are very strong. But these clones aren't that bright and don't understand their power. Truthfully, they don't understand much.

Clone Regan slowly pulls her hand way back and then slams it into the window with all her force.

CRASH!

Glass shatters and everybody inside the center screams as they cover themselves from the shards of glass raining down. The day care—where the residents of Cauldron's Cove trust their children to be kept safe—has erupted into screams, cries, and general mayhem.

"Regan!" the employee cries out, as she studies the cuts on her arms from the broken glass. "What have you done?"

So yeah, things aren't looking great for Real Regan, either.

~~~~~~~~~

Let's not forget about Bennett, as he certainly would be very, very offended to be left out.

Even his clone.

We find Clone Bennett walking—but with a slight limp—farther down on Witches' Way. He isn't fazed as sirens wail and police cars race past him down two blocks to where Clone Regan had just been. He peers into the windows of all the stores, studying the different witchy items—brooms, cauldrons, cloaks—with a confused look.

"Dude!" Max, one of Real Bennett's friends, calls out to him.

Clone Bennett tilts his head in response.

"I was just going into Worts, Sports, 'n Spells to get some new kicks. Wanna come?"

Clone Bennett grunts in reply.

"So, what's up?" Max asks as Clone Bennett follows. "I've got— Are you limping, dude? Did you hurt yourself? We've got a game coming up and Coach will not be happy if you can't play."

Clone Bennett simply grunts.

Not a big talker, Clone Bennett.

"I know, right?" Max continues as they enter the store. He goes over to the baseball card display. "I've got to get some new ones to catch up to Jimmy's collection."

Clone Bennett picks up a slim rectangular package of baseball cards. And then puts it in his pocket.

"Dude, stop!" Max hisses. "What do you think you're doing?"

Clone Bennett puts another package in his pants pocket, then turns around and falls backward.

Not a graceful fella, Clone Bennett.

While falling, he knocks over a huge display, causing a variety of sports balls to go in every direction.

"Hey!" a store employee runs toward them, jumping over soccer balls, baseballs, and basketballs.

"Put the cards back!" Max whispers in an angry, low voice. "Now!"

Clone Bennett responds by—*anybody have a guess?*—grunting. He exits the shop, leaving Max to profusely apologize to the frenzied store employee. Clone Bennett aimlessly wanders down Witches'

Way before turning on Coven Court. Where we find the other clones, all wandering without a real place to go.

But around another corner, quickly approaching, are the four students walking with a lot of purpose. And a plan.

But they have no idea what—or who—they're about to run into.

13

Have you ever been told by an adult that reading something fun—like a graphic novel or silly book—was a waste of your time? That you'd be better off reading something *important* and *literary*? And most likely *super boring*?

Well, next time you get judged for your reading material, tell that person that it could perhaps someday *save lives*.

As Darius is about to prove.

While Sofia Vargas knows a lot about nonfiction and being bossy, she has nothing on Darius when it comes to the fantastical. Zombies? Mummies? Witches? Superheroes? Darius could teach a class on them.

In fact, he's doing it right now.

"Really? That's so interesting," Sofia says to him. "You know a lot about witches. I've always looked down on witches' stories as simply the town conjuring—excuse my pun—tourists. I never believed witches were real. Maybe I can borrow some of your comic books?"

"Yeah, totally." Darius nods his head in excitement. "My buddies and I always talk about the latest issues over lunch if you ever want to join—"

"That won't be necessary," Sofia replies with a twitch of her nose, while Regan perks up.

While Regan wouldn't want to read any scary stories—this is enough drama for her *thankyouverymuch*—she would like an invitation to sit with Darius at lunch. Or even Sofia. She'd even sit with Bennett if he wasn't friends with Stu and Maisy.

"But this could help us," Sofia says.

"Are you serious?" Bennett asks as the group walks away from the library. "You're going to base our plan on stuff written in some comic?"

Sofia stops walking and looks pointedly at him. "Do *you* have a better idea?"

Bennett replies with silence.

"Yes, that's what I thought." Sofia continues to walk, inching ever so close to the intersection where *you know who* are.

Only a few feet away at this point . . .

Almost there . . .

Darius's phone rings. It's his mother.

Uh-oh.

Remember how the lady in the last chapter said she was going to call Darius's mother?

Of course you do.

Darius picks up the phone, a smile on his face. "Hey, Mom."

That smile quickly vanishes as he hears his mom's angry tone. "Darius Reginald Washington—" Oomph, when a parent uses your full name, it's never a good sign. "What on *earth* has gotten into you?"

"What do you—" a confused Darius starts, but is cut off.

He holds out his phone as his mom's loud voice blasts out so every-body can hear. "Do *not* play dumb with me. Helen Harris just called and told me that you ruined her picnic, taking a toy from her baby and then stomping all over their food with some friend."

"Wait, what? I was at the library!" Darius protests, because he *was* at the library.

"Oh, I'm not falling for that, mister. First, you get detention, and now *this*? Do I need to remind you of how under a microscope I am? Which means *you*, my son, are to behave in a respectable way. And let me assure you, if you think *I'm* upset, just wait until I speak with your father. We did not raise our son—"

"But, Mom—" Darius tries, but she is clearly not having any of it.

"—stomping and ruining people's lovely afternoon. You are to get home right this instant. Detention is nothing compared to what's going to happen when you get here. Do you understand me?"

By the way Darius is blinking at the phone in shock, it seems he doesn't understand her at all. But in these circumstances, there is only one answer a mother wants to hear. "Yes, ma'am."

With that, his phone goes silent. His mother has hung up.

"What was that about?" Bennett asks.

Darius shakes his head slowly. "I have no idea."

"But you *were* at the library." Bennett states the obvious.

"Yeah," Regan adds. "We can go to your house and tell your mom where you really were. There were lots of witnesses." Another thing Regan knows from her parents' cop shows is how important it is to have people *corroborate* your story, which is a fancy way to say agree with you on what happened.

"I've never heard my mom this mad before. I just don't understand why Mrs. Harris would lie about seeing me." Darius is slumped over in defeat. He starts dragging his feet as they are only inches away from the turn into Coven Court.

Sofia's nose perks up, and she puts her hand over her face. "What is that smell? It's disgusting." She shoots a look at Bennett.

"It wasn't me!" he protests. "Honest!"

"Yeah, I've heard that before." Sofia pinches her nose.

Darius ignores the bickering future stepsiblings. "I don't get it. There has to be some sort of explanation about what happened in the square. Maybe it was someone else, but who—" Darius starts right as they finally turn the corner.

And come face-to-face with their smelly clones.

The four kids are frozen as they take in the not-quite-right versions of themselves.

And the four clones turn to see their inspirations.

"Ah, should we run?" Regan asks as she takes an unsteady step away from her clone.

But as she studies Clone Regan, Real Regan doesn't think she looks *that* threatening. Clone Regan is in gray sweats instead of one of Real Regan's usual bright dresses. In fact, all the clone kids are in gray sweatsuits. Guess Ms. Stein didn't have time to go shopping for them. Which makes sense, since being a mad scientist must take up a lot of her time.

"They don't look scary," Sofia says as she narrows her eyes at the clones.

"But they reek." Bennett states the obvious. "Told you it wasn't me, Sof."

"It's Sofia." She pauses as she takes in the mindless shuffling and open mouths of the clones. "They look pretty harmless and, to be honest, a little lost."

Regan can't help but agree, since Bennett's clone is currently walking into a tree, while Darius's keeps bumping into a parking sign. But still, they are clones. Of them.

Can this day get any worse? Regan can't help but wonder.

(Oh, it can.)

"I can't believe it," Darius says as he takes a cautious step toward his clone. Then it's as if a light bulb goes off in his head. "Hey! Wait a second, *he* ruined the picnic! That's the only explanation, and once my—" Then Darius's face falls. "But there's no way my mom is going to believe me."

(Yeah, I'd never suggest using the it-was-my-clone excuse with a parent.)

Regan thinks back to how important evidence is in the cop shows. And the best evidence is often visual. "I know!" She grabs her phone and starts taking pictures of the clones. "This is the proof you need to convince your mother it wasn't you!"

"You're right," Darius exclaims as he also starts snapping away.

Sofia and Bennett do the same, but while keeping a safe distance from these . . . creatures. It's only Sofia who eventually starts to approach her clone.

"Fascinating." Sofia gets in her clone's scrunched-up face. She pokes. She prods. Clone Sofia scowls in return. She then goes over to Clone Bennett, who is now eating a leaf. "I see he was given your intelligence," she says with a snort.

Clone Bennett turns to Sofia and grunts.

"I actually prefer this one." Because of course she does. "He even smells better than you."

Bennett frowns. "Aw, come on, Sof!"

"It's Sofia."

"Well, maybe *your* clone can be my stepsister, then." Bennett folds his arms across his chest.

"Fine by me."

Regan takes a timid step toward her clone, who tilts her head, like she recognizes Regan. Real Regan doesn't like how sad Clone Regan looks. And scared. Does *she* really look like that? Regan *is* a little scared and sad. But she thought she was hiding it pretty well.

"Hi," Regan says timidly to her clone. "Are you okay?"

"Lalaaaalaaaaalaaaaa," Clone Regan sings back.

Regan wishes she could be brave enough to sing loudly in front of others.

Maybe her clone could try out for the choir! Even though her voice is a little off. And wobbly. And not that great.

But Clone Regan doesn't seem to care. She keeps singing. "Lalaaaaalaaaaaa!"

Bennett shakes his head as he turns back toward the entrance of Coven Court, in case he needs a quick getaway. "Okay, these things creep me out. I don't care if they're harmless or not. It's all just wrong. And can you *not*, Sofia?" Bennett scowls as Sofia keeps flicking her finger against Clone Bennett's head.

Darius keeps circling his. "I wish *this* guy could go home and get my punishment from my parents."

"That's what I was thinking," Regan says softly so nobody can hear her. What it would be like to have someone help her with everything she has to do. Maybe then she'd have time to sing and have friends and get to just be Regan instead of the babysitter, the cleaner, and the errand girl.

"That's it!" Sofia exclaims, causing Clone Bennett to grunt loudly in reply. "This works out perfectly. We need to go to Ms. Stein's when she's not at home, so the best time to do it is when we know for sure that she won't be there. Say, when she's at work."

"But wait, she's working when we're supposed to be at school,"

Regan reminds everybody. "We can't skip school. We're already in so much trouble!"

"Oh, you're right, Sofia," Darius says, ignoring Regan's very important point.

"Of course I am," Sofia replies, because of course she does.

"Right about what?" Bennett asks.

"We can send these clones to school in our place," Darius answers.

"Oh, come on! There's no way anybody is going to believe that—that—that *thing* is me!" Bennett says as he points to Clone Bennett, who is busy smelling a parking meter.

Right at that moment, Bennett's phone pings with a text from his friend Jimmy. *Dude, Max told me you stole baseball cards? Not cool. Is that why you're in detention?*

"What?" Bennett says as he reads the text. "I'd never steal— *Oh no.*"

Yeah, so much for people not believing the clone could be him.

"You stole something!" Bennett scolds his clone, who grunts in reply before putting some grass in his mouth. "Besides the fact that hideous thing doesn't look anything like me, are we forgetting that it also smells awful?"

"Again, an improvement," Sofia replies.

At that burn, Bennett takes a not-so-subtle sniff at his armpits. He smells waaaaay better than that *thing*. "Come on, Sof!"

"It's Sofia."

"Okay, then." The corner of Bennett's lips turns up, like he has something over his future stepsister. "Don't you think people will notice you're wearing sweats and not your usual uniform?"

You may be thinking, *Uniform? Sofia wears a uniform?*

Remember a long, long time ago in a chapter far, far away (chapter eight, to be exact), when I mentioned Sofia's uniform? See, Sofia wears the exact same thing—a black T-shirt and jeans—every day.

Every day.

Both Darius and Regan curiously lean in. There are many theories around Caldron's Cove Elementary about Sophia's choice of clothes: She's color-blind, she's poor, she has no taste in fashion, she's making some kind of political statement, she's protesting something, etc.

There's only one person who has ever guessed right.

And that just happened to be Darius's tech-obsessed friend Cole. On the first day of school, Cole told them he had read that the dude who invented the iPhone always wore the same thing so he didn't waste any time or brain energy deciding what to wear each morning.

Which is *exactly* why Sofia wears the same thing every day.

Not like it's anybody's business. Just like how Regan always wears bright colors after her aunt once told her she should wear black, since it was slimming. Again, why should Regan have to hide who she is? Give her all the colorful prints.

"So?" Bennett presses Sofia. "What do you think people are going to say when your clone shows up not wearing jeans and a black tee?"

Sofia shrugs. "I'm more concerned about the fact that our teacher is seeking revenge on the entire town and we're the only ones who can stop it."

The smug smile is wiped off Bennett's face. I mean, Sofia does have a pretty good point.

"Okay, okay," Regan begins before taking a deep breath. "I'll admit that it would be nice to have a clone do all the things for me that I don't want to do. But this isn't right. This is lying. We can't skip school."

"Listen, Regan, I get it," Darius says. "I'd never skip school. It *is* wrong. And since my mom is mayor, I don't get to make mistakes like other people. *But* what do you think is going to happen to us if we *do* go to school tomorrow? We have no idea what Ms. Stein is going to do next."

"Don't you think she'll recognize the clones?" Regan argues. "Bennett's right about Sofia's clothing. And I'd never wear sweats." Regan swishes the skirt of her bright yellow floral dress.

"We just need less than an hour, and by the time she—" Sofia begins before a high-pitched whistle sounds off, causing the clones to start shuffling back toward Witches' Way.

"What is that?" Regan looks around. "Where is that noise coming from?"

"It must be how Ms. Stein controls them," Darius replies before his eyes get wide. "Which means she might be nearby. Quick! Hide!"

The four duck behind a large tree and watch as the clones disappear around the corner.

"So here's the plan," Sofia begins. "Bennett and I will wait for Ms. Stein to leave her house and then we'll sneak the clones to school to take our place."

"Regan and I will then search the house while we wait for you to return," Darius offers, despite a not-too-pleased Regan beside him.

"And then the four of us will figure out how to stop Ms. Stein and save the town," Sofia finishes.

"Sound good?" Darius says. He puts his hand in the center. This time Sofia is quick to follow, with a less enthusiastic Regan behind her.

"Oh yeah," Bennett replies sarcastically as he puts his hand in. "We'll just skip school, break into a teacher's house, and save the town. What could possibly go wrong?"

(Quite a lot, actually.)

"Call it sibling bonding," Sofia replies as Bennett groans, sounding very similar to his clone.

They have a plan.

But first, they have to go home and face their parents after their clones wreaked havoc on the town.

Yep, I told you things would get scary.

14

Nobody ever said saving your hometown would be easy.

Especially when parents get involved.

Our poor heroes. Here they are with the weight of trying to clear their names and save their school from being overrun by clones and *now* they're in big trouble for something they didn't do.

Now, we could watch each one get yelled at when they got home, but for their sake—and ours, because *yikes*—here is a basic rundown of what happened.

As I'm sure you have never, ever been in trouble, innocent reader, the following will obviously be something you have never, ever dealt with.

Parent: WE NEED TO HAVE A TALK, [insert first name]. YOU SIT DOWN RIGHT THERE AND EXPLAIN YOURSELF.

Kid: I—

Parent: I CAN'T BELIEVE YOU WOULD DO SOMETHING LIKE THIS! WHAT ON EARTH WERE YOU THINKING?

Kid: It wasn't—

Parent: I DON'T WANT TO HEAR IT! YOU NEED TO EXPLAIN YOURSELF, [insert full, middle, *and* last name].

Kid: But you just said you didn't want to hear—

PARENT: DID YOU NOT THINK ABOUT HOW THIS WOULD AFFECT THE B&B / THE VISITORS CENTER / MY REELECTION?

Kid: But I—

Parent: THEN WHY DID [witness] SAY YOU [did something they certainly didn't do].

Kid: Well, I—

Parent: I SAID, EXPLAIN YOURSELF!

Kid: I'm trying!

(*Parents, am I right?*)

Parent: I AM WAITING!

Kid: It wasn't me! Honest! And I know this is going to sound crazy, but it was a clone.

(Remember how I said don't use the it-was-my-clone excuse? Well, you're about to find out why.)

Parent: WHAT DID YOU JUST SAY?

Kid: It was a clone.

Parent: A WHAT?

Kid: A clone! See!

At this point, the kid shows their parent/s the photo they took earlier of their clone.

Parent: WHAT IS THIS? A PHOTO OF YOU? WHAT DOES THIS PROVE? DO YOU SERIOUSLY EXPECT ME TO BELIEVE THIS IS A CLONE? I WAS NOT BORN YESTERDAY!

Kid: Can you please stop yelling—

Parent: OH, YOU DO *NOT* GET TO TELL ME WHAT I CAN OR CANNOT DO. THAT IS NOT HOW THIS WORKS. I DID NOT RAISE . . .

And it goes on and on and on like this for a very, very long time. Insert extremely unfair and unreasonable punishment.

However, this just gives each of our young heroes more reason to get inside Ms. Stein's house and find a way to stop Ann Wilder's curse.

Not just for the town of Cauldron's Cove, but to prove to their parents that they didn't ruin a picnic / steal baseball cards / break a window.

15

As we are all more than aware, the kids are in trouble. Big trouble. With their parents. With their school. With their science teacher.

You know what could get them into even *more* trouble? Breaking and entering into Ms. Stein's house.

It would be pure insanity for them to even try it, right?

Welp, that is precisely what we find our foursome doing the next morning.

Now, I'm sure you think you know these kids by now. Have them all figured out. Might even think you can tell the story better.

Well, let's just see. Would you like to guess which kid is currently picking the lock to Ms. Stein's front door?

Did you guess Sofia, since she's so smart and seems to know everything?

Or maybe Darius, since he's so well-read?

Or perhaps Bennett, since he talks (and often plays) a big game?

Well, if you guessed any of those, you are wrong! WRONG!

Which is a good thing, because I can keep my job. *Phew*.

You see, it's sweet I-don't-want-to-get-in-trouble Regan who is going to get them inside.

Now, Regan didn't do anything to get into detention, but this, *this* could land her in juvie.

Visions of wearing an orange jumpsuit and being behind bars flash through Regan's head as she sits down next to the front doorknob of Ms. Stein's house. She breaks out a ███████ to ███████ and ███████ while ███████ and then ███████.

Now, dear reader, you may have noticed that my publisher has decided to black out some of the text. They apparently don't want me to tell you how to break into someone's house. (*How rude!*) It was something like "What on earth are you thinking? You'll be held accountable, yada, yada, blah, blah, blah . . ."

I'm sure I'm not the only one who blanks out when adults are being *so adult*.

Anyhoo, between guests at the B&B often locking the key in their rooms and her younger siblings accidentally locking themselves in the bathroom, Regan has had to pick a lock or two. Like with most questionable things, she learned it on the internet. Since Regan can remember better by watching something be done instead of reading about it or verbally being told, she watched a video.

Several times. Things seem to click into place when she sees something get done.

Click!

And just like that, the lock releases and Regan triumphantly opens the front door to Ms. Stein's.

"Not bad," Bennett says with a nod of respect.

"Yes, very impressive," Sofia agrees.

That's right. Sofia and Bennett agree on something for once.

"And this was genius," Bennett adds as he holds up the child leashes that Regan brought along. Regan has needed them when she's been in charge of keeping her younger siblings from wandering off whenever her family goes to the grocery store, mall, or . . . basically anywhere.

Sofia takes the leashes and heads inside Ms. Stein's house with Bennett while Regan and Darius keep watch outside.

"I can't believe we're actually doing this," Regan says as she wraps her arms around herself.

Darius nods along. "Yeah, but what else can we do? And no matter what happens, I've got your back."

"Same," Regan says with a small smile, as a blush starts to creep on her pale face. As much as the whole potential life of crime and being locked away for life scares her, she likes being part of this group. Knowing that Darius would have Regan's back if she needed him.

Out the door comes Bennett pulling on the leashes as the four clones shuffle behind him. Real Bennett grunts as he drags the four clones across the street. The clones appear to be just as difficult to wrangle as Regan's siblings. Clone Sofia walks in the opposite direction of everybody else. Clone Regan keeps stopping to sing "Laaaalaaaalaaaaa!" to the pumpkins that line the sidewalk. Clone Darius just randomly stops in the middle of the street. And Clone Bennett keeps walking into trees.

Not the most cooperative, these clones.

"Come on!" Real Bennett groans as he yanks on the separate leashes to (unsuccessfully) try to get them in an orderly line.

Sofia stands in front of Darius and Regan with a serious look on her face. "Okay. If all goes well, we'll be back in twelve and a half minutes. In the meantime, make sure you keep your gloves on and don't break anything."

"You got it." Darius enters the house without a second glance at Regan, who is hesitating outside. Yes, Regan already broke a law by picking Ms. Stein's lock, *but* going into Ms. Stein's house seems like a bigger deal.

"One more thing," Sofia says as she pauses at the crosswalk. "In case there is any kind of lock with a code, Ms. Stein's birthday is eleven, twenty-five, ninety-seven if you need anything with numbers." With that, Sofia gives Regan a nod and hurries after Bennett and the unruly clones.

"Um, wait!" Regan pats her empty pockets. They were told not to bring anything in order to avoid accidentally leaving something behind. Usually Regan has a tiny notebook in her backpack to write down directions, numbers, anything that might easily get jumbled in her head. "Sofia!"

It's too late. Sofia is already down the street.

Regan repeats to herself, *Eleven, twenty—was it five? Or twenty-seven? Was Ms. Stein born in . . .*

Oh no. No.

Regan starts panicking. She can't mess this up for the group. But it's hard for her to keep numbers straight in her head. Even if she writes them down, she needs to be very careful and make sure she puts them in the right order. That usually requires her to verbally repeat them back. But now . . .

Eleven, twenty . . . something, and ninety-five. Or ninety-seven? Drat. Regan groans.

"Are you coming in?" Darius calls out from the doorway. "We don't want to be caught lingering. You look really suspicious right now."

Regan glances around the empty neighborhood, but knows Darius is right. It just takes one person to see them and it's all over.

But . . .

"Maybe we don't need to go in," Regan reasons. "I mean, that alone proves that something isn't right." She points to the scene down the street of the clones walking in opposite directions with Bennett and Sofia dragging them along.

"Come on," Darius replies from the doorway before disappearing farther into Ms. Stein's house.

Leaving Regan alone. Again. She bites her nails, already down to her skin. How could anybody see Sofia and Bennett right now and think this isn't odd?

But then she remembers how mad her parents were last night. Accusing her of smashing the day care's window. And how they didn't believe her when she tried to explain what was really going on. She told her parents the truth, the whole truth. They replied by being disappointed in her.

No, the only way for the foursome to end this is to do it themselves.

Regan takes a step inside Ms. Stein's house.

That's one small step for Regan, one giant leap into a possible life of crime.

Regan's mind starts spiraling. *Wait. What was Ms. Stein's birthday again? It was November. Yes, and twenty-something and sometime in the nineties. That should at least help somewhat.*

She hopes. Oh, how she hopes.

If saving the town comes down to Regan remembering numbers, it will prove everybody who has refused to be her partner in class right.

"It's in here!" Darius calls from down the hallway.

Not like anybody needs to be told. White light flashes down the hallway, like a severe lightning storm, but inside. Even with the curtains closed and all the lights off, the dining room is blindingly bright. At the center of the dining room table is a big metal ball, shooting sparks and light from all directions. There are drawings and equations written on the wall and on practically every surface of the table. There are also a few sharp knives and one very, very long and thick needle. Next to the table is a large glass cylinder filled with a light green goo.

Darius points to the goo. "That's probably what she used to make the clones."

But Regan isn't listening. She's too busy trying to remember all the numbers.

"Regan?"

"Oh, sorry!" Regan bites down on her lip. "Did you, ah, hear the number that Sofia said before—"

"November twenty-fifth, ninety-seven," Darius replies without hesitation.

Regan feels both relief that Darius knows it, and also that pinching feeling she gets when she remembers how easy things like numbers and verbal instructions are for other people. Darius is also one of the best spellers in class. He's usually in the finals of the annual spelling bee with Sofia.

Not Regan. She has to close her eyes and shut them tight trying to picture how to spell a word, and she usually gets it wrong. She's always out in the first round.

Her bottom lip quivers.

Darius takes a step closer to her. "Hey, are you okay? I know this is scary and all, but we're so close to figuring this all out."

"I'm only going to let you all down," Regan admits. "I can't remember a simple date. It gets scrambled in my head. I'm so stupid."

"No, you're not, Regan." Darius crosses his arms, like he means business. "Look, not everybody's brain works the same. That doesn't mean you're stupid, it makes you special. And that's not a bad thing to be. You know how much I love superheroes?"

Regan nods. Darius is basically a walking superhero advertisement. He lives in Marvel and comic book T-shirts and sweatshirts. His head is always buried in a graphic novel during quiet reading.

"Well, that's because superheroes are different," Darius continues.

"Their powers make them the *opposite* of normal. I think that's what truly makes them super, that they're able to do amazing things despite being seen by others as different or weird."

"Really?" Regan sniffs.

"Yeah. Peter Parker gets bullied at school because he's super smart and a bit of a nerd. People don't know he's Spider-Man. That's pretty good company to be in, huh?"

Regan nods her head, although she'd rather be compared to Wonder Woman.

But Darius is right. What makes superheroes special is that they have moments just like Regan is having now. Moments when they need to be brave, even if they're scared.

Regan nods her head as if she's agreeing with me (which she is because she *is* smart). "Okay, what should we do?"

"Gloves on?" Darius holds up his hands, which are covered with black knit gloves.

Regan shows off the purple-and-yellow mittens her grandmother knit her for Christmas last year. Probably not the best accessory for rummaging through someone's stuff, but it's all she had. Sofia made it clear that they couldn't leave fingerprints behind in case the cops were called in. *The cops.*

Regan takes a big gulp. This is such a bad idea.

Darius bends down to a stack of boxes and containers near a wall. "Let's go through these and see what's— GAH!" Darius cries out as he falls backward.

Regan rushes over to find a glass container with . . . oh my goodness, is that a *human head*? At least it looks like a head, but it's gloopy. (Yes, that is a technical term: *gloopy*, from the Latin *gloopus*.) The head doesn't have much shape. It looks like a doll's head that's been left out on a super sunny and hot day.

There's another container next to it that has . . . guts? Or organs?

Gross.

But we're just getting started.

Because Regan and Darius aren't alone.

BANG! BANG! BANG!

"What was that?" Darius looks up to the ceiling.

Regan is too terrified to reply. First there's a head in a container and now there's something—or someone—upstairs.

(Believe me, they do *not* want to know what Ms. Stein has hidden upstairs. But they'll soon find out. And you can bet it won't be good.)

Regan and Darius are frozen looking at the ceiling, wondering what's going to happen next.

"Okay!" Sofia says as she storms through the door, causing both Darius and Regan to yelp. "Yes, yes, I realize we're a couple minutes late. *Someone* had an issue due to his delicate ego."

Bennett walks in with a frown on his face. "I saw my buddies just accept my clone. They didn't even bat an eye." He shakes his head . . . and then takes a sniff of his armpits.

"We have more important things to focus on right now," Sofia replies as she puts on plastic gloves, the kind detectives use, because of course she has those. She looks at the drawings around the room, which have the same kind of frantic scrawls like in Ms. Stein's notebook. Sofia points at the vat of goo. "Okay. I believe Ms. Stein combined our DNA with this substance to create the clones, which then came to life with that." She then points at the electricity.

"I don't get it," Bennett says.

"What a shock," Sofia says with a shake of her head.

"Come on, Sof!"

"It's Sofia."

Bennett throws his arms in the air. "How are we supposed to understand any of this with what we've learned in science class? Are we really to believe my spit and some goo created that—that—that *thing*! Which, for the record, I do not look or smell like. At all."

"What are we going to do, then?" Regan asks. "Can we just take pictures and show them to our parents to prove that Ms. Stein is up to something? Or maybe call the police?"

"No!" Darius protests. "They'll lock us up for breaking into her house. Besides, Ms. Stein could argue that it's all part of her book research."

"Authors don't have evil lairs!" Regan fires back.

(Well, *some* of us don't.)

Regan gestures around the room. "This has to be enough proof. Or we'll go to school and then people will see the clones and us together, and that will just prove that Ms. Stein—"

"Yes?" comes a voice from the front door.

The four look over to see none other than Ms. Stein.

And she looks mad. Really, really mad.

16

Wow. You turned that page pretty fast, huh?

Curious about what's about to happen now that Ms. Stein has caught the kids inside her house?

Well, I won't keep you.

No, I believe time is of the essence, and to waste any more of your precious reading time before telling you what's happening would be quite rude.

I am many things—clever, hilarious, cheese-filled, adorable—but I am *not* rude.

No, not me. I was a particularly well-behaved child in my youth. In fact, as family legend has it, when I was born on a warm July morning—

Whoa there. Are you mad at me right now? Why? It's not like—

Oh yeah. Our heroes. I should probably get back to their story, huh?

Right. *Ahem.*

As you may recall, Ms. Stein does not look happy. *Wait a second.*
Now her lips are turning up ever so slightly as she takes in the four
students in her dining room. She looks . . . thrilled.

That can't be good.

"Did you think I wouldn't recognize my own creations?" Ms. Stein
asks with an unsettling laugh.

Darius gestures around her dining room, his hand slightly shaking. "Do *you* think this isn't enough to prove to people what you're
really up to?"

Ms. Stein takes a step closer to Darius, who in return scoots back
to the far wall. "I believe all of your parents would be a lot more concerned about their children not only skipping school, but breaking
into a teacher's house."

Hmm. Ms. Stein does have a point.

"How will this look for your mother's reelection campaign when it
gets out her son has no regard for law and order, Darius?"

Darius's shoulders slump slightly in reply.

"And Regan, would people trust their valuables when they stay at
your parents' Bed and Boofast now?"

Regan's chin trembles again. She can't help but feel that all she's
been doing lately is disappointing people. Her siblings were almost

banned from day care after her clone broke the window, and now her parents' business could suffer.

Ms. Stein continues, "Nevertheless, I should really be thanking you. You have made this easier on me. I didn't even need to set a trap. You've set one for yourselves quite nicely."

She takes a whistle from her pocket and blows.

STOMP.

STOMP.

STOMP.

The entire house rattles as something makes its way down the stairs.

STOMP.

STOMP.

STOMP.

The noise is coming closer. And what's that they're hearing?

Is that grunting? Isn't Clone Bennett at school with the rest of the clones?

The four heroes gasp in unison as a *thing* enters the dining room.

It's a . . . monster. Sort of. This is a different kind of clone. We've already seen Ms. Stein's first attempts at cloning with the not-quite-right clones of each of the kids. But this—this *thing* is her masterpiece.

A clone created from all four of the students. It has Regan's size, Darius's height times two, Sofia's scowl, and Bennett's face. It has a darker greenish tint than the other clones.

"Uuuuhhhh," the monster calls out.

And it apparently also possesses Clone Bennett's limited vocabulary.

The monster takes one, two, three steps closer to the students, who are now backed into a corner in the dining room. There is only one way out, and Ms. Stein is blocking it.

"You children have been more trouble than you're worth," Ms. Stein says. "Which is exactly why these clones are needed. They obey." She holds up her whistle. "And your replacements are at school getting along quite well. Oh, don't you worry. I still have some work to do to perfect them. But now, now I have unlimited resources." She gestures at the students, then cocks her eyebrow in victory.

Unlimited resources? Regan's hand automatically goes to the back of her head, even though she has a feeling Ms. Stein is after more than just a few strands of her hair. By looking around the table at the needles and knives and goo, she can only hope she'll get out of the house with only pulled hair.

If she'll be able to escape.

The monster is only a foot away from our heroes and, wow, the stink emanating from it is something else.

Think your weeks-old gym socks, a tuna fish sandwich that has been left in the sun, the stinkiest cheese in the world, a huge burp, and broccoli. Just regular broccoli. And you're only halfway to the monster's smell.

Ms. Stein approaches the lightning orb as if she's drawn to it. She stares at it and whispers, "Are you pleased with my work? I've done everything you've asked."

Sofia and Darius exchange a look. Yeah, I also think that seems . . . weird. But then again, *none of this is normal*!

"This town will rue the day it vexed you. You will have your revenge!" Ms. Stein lets out what could best be described as an evil cackle before turning back to the monster. "Lock them up. I've got a class to teach." Her bloodshot eyes are extra crazed as she gives the kids one more unsettling look before turning her back on them and walking out the front door.

Leaving them alone with the monster.

The monster takes a step closer, and they can feel its hot, gross breath on their faces. It towers over the group at nearly ten feet tall.

Its shoulders are wide, like it wouldn't be able to pass through a door-frame without turning.

"Wait for my sign and then run," Sofia whispers. "It can only catch one of us."

Bennett steps in front of Sofia, separating her from the monster. "Let me do it. He can chase me."

"What?" Sofia replies in surprise. "Are you serious?"

"Of course. I'm the fastest out of us. He'll never be able to catch me."

"And there's that ego." Sofia pushes Bennett aside. "I can more than handle myself." She takes a step toward the monster, who grins at her with yellow, crooked teeth.

Then Sofia kicks the monster in the shins with all her might.

"Ah . . ." she calls out as she takes a few steps to the left, a slight limp in her right foot.

The monster looks down at Sofia unfazed. "Uuuuhhhhhh."

So that didn't go according to plan.

The monster's black eyes follow Sofia as she moves closer to the dining room table. Then Sofia takes one of the dining room chairs, picks it up, and hurls it at the monster.

Who, in turn, swats it away like a fly.

The monster grunts in annoyance. Like it finally realizes Sofia is attacking it and, no surprise, it is *not* happy about it.

"RUN!" Sofia calls out as the monster takes a step toward her.

You don't need to tell Regan twice. With the monster distracted by Sofia, she and Darius bolt out of the room and through the front door. To safety.

Phew.

But the future stepsiblings are still trapped inside.

Bennett runs up to the monster and punches it in the shoulder. "Come on, come after me!" The monster turns fully to Bennett, allowing Sofia to slip away toward the front door.

"Let's do this!" Bennett challenges the monster. Bennett turns around with a confident grin on his face. He starts to follow Sofia out of the house . . . then BAM! Bennett trips over the table leg and crashes down onto the floor.

Huh, it seems Real Bennett isn't that graceful of a fella, either.

Sofia's hand is on the doorknob. Regan and Darius are safely across the street, both staring at the house with fear in their eyes.

The monster grabs onto Bennett's leg and picks him up like he's a rag doll.

"Go, Sofia! Run!" Bennett cries out as he dangles upside down. "Just go!"

Sofia is of course going to do what Bennett says.

(*Ha! Kidding!* We all know better at this point, right?)

Instead of listening to Bennett and getting herself to safety, Sofia pulls her hand away from the doorknob.

"What are you doing?" Bennett calls out in pain as the monster grips his leg tighter. "Go!"

Sofia takes a step closer to the monster. "No. I know how to handle myself with this beast. *You* should go."

"What?" Bennett twists himself around in the air.

"Come at me!" Sofia taunts the monster.

The beast turns to Sofia, who now has the front door wide open. The monster takes a few steps toward her.

"Don't!" Bennett protests. "Just go!"

Sofia in turn walks even *closer* to the monster. She narrows her eyes and leans in. "If I'm correct, and we both know I am, your brain is based on me. So you know that I'm a much better match for you than Bennett. Put him down. Take me instead."

"Are you serious?" Bennett shouts. "You can't possibly—"

But Bennett is cut off. The monster drops him near the door with a thud, then immediately grabs Sofia by the arm.

Bennett shakes his head as he stands up, like he's trying to make sense of what's going on.

"Get out!" Sofia says as she pushes Bennett out the door with her free arm.

"Please don't do this, Sof," he begs as tears well up in his eyes.

"It's Sofia!" She slams the front door in Bennett's face.

Locking him safely outside and her inside with the monster.

17

Ah, that was a bit of an unexpected turn of events, huh?

Even I got a little emotional when Sofia sacrificed herself for Bennett. That's right, for *Bennett*, her future stepbrother, who she doesn't really seem to like. Who seems to annoy her to no end.

Could it be that we have Sofia all wrong?

Confession time, dear reader: Even *I* am a little worried about Sofia. Not only because of her seemingly out-of-character sacrifice, but for her safety. Sofia may be smart, but that monster is something else entirely.

And none of it is good.

The remaining members of the group—Darius, Bennett, and Regan—go to Darius's house for safety after escaping Ms. Stein's house. Luckily, Darius not only lives the farthest away from Ms. Stein, he has a sweet tree house to hide away from Ms. Stein, the monsters, and most importantly, their parents.

Bennett is currently pacing around the tree house. "What are we going to do?" he says, collapsing on one of the beanbags in the corner.

"We have to go back there," Darius replies, while Regan falls onto the other beanbag.

Bennett shakes his head in shock. "I can't believe Sofia did that."

"Yeah, she sacrificed herself like a true hero," Darius says with a nod of respect.

"No," Regan replies. "She did what any sibling would've done."

Bennett looks at Regan in surprise. "What do you mean?"

"Well." Regan wrings her hands. She's been a nervous wreck since well . . . she first walked into detention two days ago. "I would've done the same thing if it was one of my brothers or sisters trapped with that monster. You may think Sofia doesn't care about you with the . . . ah . . ."

"Constant mocking and scowling?" Bennett finishes for her. "Because she *doesn't* care about me. She *hates* me."

"She wouldn't have done that for someone she didn't care about."

"That's true," Darius agrees.

"Wait a second. Just wait one second." Bennett puts his head in his hands. "Are you saying Sofia actually likes me?"

Regan pauses for a moment. "No, I think she *loves* you. You're siblings. You're family."

"I mean, we will be in a couple weeks, but she's always—"

"Herself," Darius interrupts.

Bennett laughs for a second. "Yeah, I guess. I mean, here's the thing that I don't think I could ever admit to Sofia because she'd be . . . Sofia. But I really like her." Bennett pauses for a moment. He opens his mouth, closes it, opens it again. It's like for a moment he's unsure if he should admit the whole truth. But then he looks at Darius and Regan, who he's already been through so much with. He can share this, too. "Okay, here's the deal: I love Sofia. She's my sister. It doesn't matter that we're not blood related. And I can't help but feel protective of her. You know how she gets."

Both Regan and Darius nod because I think at this point there isn't a person in Cauldron's Cove—or a reader of this book—who doesn't know how Sofia gets.

"Yeah, she's always wound so tightly," Bennett continues. "I just want her to know she's going to be okay . . . and then I just up and leave her behind, right when she needed me the most. I'm just like my dad."

That's when Bennett Norland, Mr. Cool, lets out a sob. Like, an actual tear streaks down his face and he gets all snotty as he doesn't fight back his sadness.

At that outburst, Darius stands up and starts walking around the cramped tree house, pretending to study the comics that line the wall.

Boys, am I right?

No surprise it's Regan who sits down next to Bennett. "Do you want to talk about it?"

Okay, I gave you proper warning when things were going to get scary, but you should be aware that things are about to get pretty emotional. Get those tissues ready!

"My dad up and leaves my mom and me when I was six. Like just walked out. We were both really hurt. I mean, how could someone who is supposed to be a father do that to their family?" Bennett sniffs. "Then Sofia and her dad come into our life and it's like a piece of the puzzle snaps into place. Sofia's dad is just this great guy and Sofia is pretty fun to have around, even when she's being insufferable. And then I abandon her."

"Sofia didn't give you much of a choice," Regan reasons. She pats Bennett on the shoulder. Her hearts tugs at what he said. She could never imagine her dad leaving. She's so grateful for her busy and chaotic family, even if they don't leave much time for Regan to simply be Regan. "Sometimes siblings have to make sacrifices for each other. If Sofia let you go, it's because she has faith in you. We all do."

"Thanks, Regan. I appreciate it and . . ." Bennett takes a shaky breath and pauses for a moment. "And I'm really sorry I didn't say anything when Stu was being a jerk at the library."

"Oh," Regan says in surprise. She's not used to people realizing they should maybe treat her a little better. She's accustomed to being someone who gets ignored or teased. There never seems to be a middle ground for Regan when it comes to her fellow students at Cauldron's Cove Elementary.

Although now that she thinks about it, it was Sofia who stood up for Regan. Hmm, maybe Regan has had Sofia wrong this entire time, as well?

Bennett kicks at the wooden floor. "Yeah, you didn't deserve that and I wasn't brave enough to say anything. I'm glad Sofia did, but it should've been me. I promise you I won't let him—or anybody—talk to you that way again. It wasn't okay."

"Thanks." Regan clears her throat, feeling a bit emotional herself.

See, I told you feelings were going to be had. Do you need a break? Get some tissues? Cry into a pint of ice cream? Pet a puppy? Hug a *sibling*?

I don't know about you, but I need less emotion right now and more doing.

Come on, people! Need I remind everybody what's at stake here? Also the teeny-tiny fact that Sofia is trapped inside an evil lair with a monster!

So let's get to it, shall we?

Bennett stands up with more confidence. "We need to come up with a plan. For Sofia."

"For Sofia," Regan agrees, and puts her hand in the center. Darius and Bennett immediately join in.

"But *how* are we going to come up with a plan without Sofia?" Bennett asks.

Darius starts pacing the room, just like Sofia does when she's trying to piece something together. "Did you notice how weird Ms. Stein was being? I mean, obviously. But when she was in her lab, she *talked* to that orb. She mentioned *revenge*. Sofia gave me that look when Ms. Stein did it. Like she knew that orb is the key."

"Okay," Regan says as she nods her head. "I can't believe I'm going to say this, but there really is only one answer. We need to break back into Ms. Stein's house, rescue Sofia, and destroy that orb."

"Exactly." Darius stops in front of a panel of one of his favorite comic books.

"Okay." Bennett pauses for a moment. "Um, do we have any idea *how* we're going to do any of that?"

Darius turns around with a smile on his lips. "As a matter of fact, I do."

18

Darius stands before Regan and Bennett. "Be honest, how do I smell?"

Now, reader, I can't verify how you personally smell at this precise moment in time. You may want to lift up your arms and take a deep sniff of your pits to make sure you aren't emitting any foul and offensive odors.

There's something you should know, though: Darius *wants* to smell bad. Really, *really* bad.

Why?

Well, who else smells really, *really* bad?

Yep.

See, as you're aware, the trio has decided they need to break back into Ms. Stein's house to get Sofia. But in order to ensure they aren't falling into any traps, one of them needs to pretend to be a clone.

And that someone is Darius.

Ergo, dude needs to stink up the place.

Bennett takes a deep whiff of Darius. His nose twitches, but he shakes his head. "Pretty bad, but not disgusting enough."

"Here." Regan hands Darius some stinky cheese that he rubs over his clothes. He then puts some hard-boiled eggs in his pockets.

"I feel like I'm an extra in a movie," Darius says as he puts on some makeup. He's using Regan's mom's face powder to dull his skin.

"This really should be me," Bennett replies as he rubs dog poo on Darius's jeans. "I'm the one who left Sofia behind."

"You didn't leave her behind," Regan reminds him. "It was a decision she made. And you're the obvious choice to save Sofia. We need an element of surprise."

"I think I'm almost ready." Darius slumps over and walks in the weird shuffle motion of his clone. "This is totally going to work."

"And I'm so ready." Bennett takes a few swings of a baseball bat.

Bennett's part of the plan is to take out that orb.

While Regan has to get them back inside by picking the lock.

"We already know Regan's got her part down," Bennett says before lightly punching her on the shoulder like he does with his bros.

Regan should feel happy that they know she won't let them down. That she's part of the team. That Bennett seems to actually respect her, but . . .

Regan frowns.

"What is it?" Bennett asks as he continues to swing the bat.

More like what *isn't* it? Yeah, Regan is helping rescue Sofia, but that tug she felt before is dragging her down. First, she disappointed her parents by getting detention. Then the mix-up at the day care. And now, *now* she's a full criminal.

But somehow, something else is bothering her.

"I know this sounds silly at this point, but I just can't believe Ms. Stein would do this to us."

"I think it's pretty clear Ms. Stein isn't really in control of what she's doing," Darius replies. "That orb is. Or whoever is controlling the orb. Which is why we need to destroy it."

Regan nods meekly. "I guess. It's just I like to believe the best of people."

"That's not a bad thing," Darius argues.

"Yeah, but it never seems to go both ways. People look at me and just assume that I'm lazy because I'm fat."

Darius nods along. "I get it. Whenever I go into a store, I get followed around because I'm Black."

Both Darius and Regan look over at Bennett.

He drops his bat. "Ah . . . yeah, so like . . . um, people just, like, assume . . . um, I think I'm just going to stop talking."

Regan and Darius just shake their heads. People look at Bennett and see a confident, good-looking guy. Must be nice to be Bennett. (And most times it is, except when his science teacher is trying to replace him.)

Regan continues, "It really hurts that my parents think I'm this irresponsible person after the clone broke that window."

"That wasn't you, just like I wasn't in the park." Darius clenches his teeth.

"I know." Regan bites her lip. "But my parents *believed* I was capable of something like that, which almost makes it worse. And now with this"—she gestures at her lock-picking tools— "I'm almost fulfilling some destiny to keep letting them down."

"You're not letting anyone down." Darius puts his hand on her shoulder. "We all got in trouble with our parents, but we're going to get Sofia out, destroy the lab, and end this. And then . . ."

Darius doesn't finish his thought, and neither Regan nor Bennett fills in what their future will hold after they leave Ms. Stein's house. *If* they even survive.

As much as they all want this to end, could they really go back to how things were before? Just four classmates (save the two future stepsiblings) who will nod to one another occasionally in the hallways.

Regan doesn't want that. She likes being part of a team. She likes that she's helpful. Even when that means she has to break a law or two.

Bennett takes a few more swings of his bat. "We need to get moving before school lets out. Do we have everything?"

Darius looks over the list he wrote, detailing the plan that came from one of his comic books, where someone covered himself in zombie guts to go undetected among the undead.

Now it's time for them to practice what Darius reads.

Darius nods confidentially. "We're ready."

Bennett pumps his fist. "Let's go save my sister and Cauldron's Cove!"

19

Brace yourself. What I'm about to tell you may come as a shock.

I know you've already seen a lot of pretty crazy stuff so far: Clones, curses, witches, parents *kissing*. But this, *this* might be the most shocking.

Ready?

Sofia Vargas appears to be super annoyed.

(That is what you call sarcasm, because *no duh* Sofia is annoyed.)

"Here I assumed you'd know how to play a simple game like chess," Sofia says to her opponent. Who just happens to be the monster that has her tied up in the living room. The monster studies the chess board that Sofia had instructed it to set up.

Sofia isn't going to let a little thing like being held hostage stop her from a stimulating game of chess.

The monster, however, isn't having any of it. It grunts before flipping the board over.

"So I take it that you don't know how to play."

The monster grunts in reply.

"Fair enough." Sofia studies the monster. Its large features should be intimidating, but since it shares Bennett's face, it's a little less so. "But you do realize that Ms. Stein is just using you, right? Since you share my DNA, *something* has to be going on in that brain of yours."

The monster grunts.

Sofia sighs. "I do have to admit, I prefer you over the real Bennett."

Guess what the monster does. Yup. Grunts.

"Okay, Bennett's not *that* bad. I'm sure there are worse step-siblings in the world. I mean, he did want to take my place, which was nice and all. But let's face it, he'd be useless in here. Not me, I've got a front-row seat to Ms. Stein's lab. You should also be aware that I have everything figured out." Because of course she does. "Now, if you could just let me go, I will free you and the other clones and this entirely inconvenient plot can be finished."

The monster blankly stares at her.

"Oh, come on!" She throws her head back in frustration. "Fine. I'm assuming that if you have some of my traits, you're just as stubborn as I can be. Not that that's bad. Better than being a pushover. So never mind. Leave me locked up. In fact I *want* to stay here and be tied up to have a conversation with a grunting beast."

The monster tilts its head at Sofia.

"Yes, it's nice to have some peace and quiet for a change. I'd love nothing more than to stay here."

This, dear reader, is what you call reverse psychology. It's when someone thinks they can convince you to do something by urging you to do the opposite.

You know what, that's something that would be difficult for someone of your intelligence to understand. In fact, *you* would be better off if you just stopped reading this book now. It's just too awesome and amazing for someone like you.

Put the book down.

Stop reading.

(If you're still reading: BUSTED! You so fell for reverse psychology. But it's totally cool. You get to keep reading the book!)

(If you stopped reading: Ah, you wouldn't be reading this, so never mind. But let me tell you, you are missing out, as things are about to get really, really good. Not like you'd know, as no one is reading this.)

Since the monster doesn't fall for Sofia's trap, she unfolds her legs in front of her and leans against the wall, settling in. "Could you be a doll and fetch me a book? Might as well get some reading in."

The monster simply grunts back.

She shakes her head. "I can't believe Ms. Stein thought she could take over the town—or at the very least the school—with you. What a waste of my precious DNA."

The front door opens and Sofia stiffens. School is still in session, so it can't be Ms. Stein—or can it? She sets her face into a hard line as if she's preparing for whoever—or whatever—she's about to come face-to-face with.

The door opens and a clone that looks like Darius shuffles in. Now, you and I know it's Real Darius, but Sofia couldn't know this. And Darius is being very convincing with all the slouching and stinking.

Darius slowly shuffles toward the monster, who stands up and approaches him. The monster gives Darius a low grunt. Darius motions his head for the monster to follow him. The monster narrows its eyes as it gets closer. Darius bristles, which is not a bad thing, since the clones are not the most graceful creatures. The monster's nose twitches as it smells Darius.

Perhaps they went a little overboard on the dog poo.

Darius opens the closet in the front hallway.

"Gaaaaahh," he growls in a low voice.

I think that means *Please get inside the closet* in clone-speak.

And wouldn't you know it, the monster actually gets into the closet—although it has to duck with its height—and squats in the middle of

Ms. Stein's coats. Darius slams the door behind the monster and locks it inside.

After taking a very deep sigh of relief, although he gags a bit, since, *wow*, does he really stink, Darius spins around to find Sofia standing up, her tied hands held out in front of her.

"Hi, Darius. Please untie me," Sofia says in a bored tone.

"What?" Darius exclaims. "How did you know it was me and not my clone?"

Sofia scoffs. "Please."

Because of course she does.

As Darius bends down to untie Sofia, she takes a whiff of his stench. "I see you've borrowed Bennett's cologne." She shakes out her hands after being freed. "I take it you didn't come alone?"

"Oh yeah, right." Darius turns around and calls out. "You can come in!"

Bennett practically knocks down the front door, carrying two baseball bats. "Sofia, we've come here to rescue you," he says with all the bravado of a superhero as he throws one of the bats to Darius.

Sofia rolls her eyes, not at all impressed.

Bennett doesn't seem to care as he runs over and wraps his future stepsister into his arms. "I'm so glad you're okay! I'm so sorry I just left you—"

"It's fine." Sofia pushes Bennett off her as she goes to the dining room table with the pulsing orb and vat of goo. "Now, let's finish this."

Darius, Regan, and Bennett stand beside her as they face the orb with a look of determination on their faces.

Darius takes a step forward, tapping his baseball bat with his hand. "Let's destroy this thing."

20

This is the moment. And by the expression of glee on Bennett's face, it looks like he can't wait to smash that orb. Not that I blame him. What with the whole being framed for shoplifting and his friends thinking he's a super stinky and clumsy *thing*.

Bennett pulls his bat back, ready to swing—

"Don't!" Sofia calls out, stopping his momentum.

"Aw, Sof!"

"It's Sofia." She shakes her head. "I know you want to release your pent-up testosterone, but this orb contains a huge charge of electricity. Did you really think you could just smash it and all would be okay? The charge could kill us all."

Yikes. I'm pretty sure the rest of them didn't think of that. Goodness, *I* didn't even think of it!

Sofia walks around the table before taking a step back and looking up at the lightning. The hair on her arms is sticking up. There's a buzzing charge around them. The closer she gets to the orb, the more her hair starts flying up.

"From what I've gathered, it seems that the night of the storm, a bolt of lightning came into Ms. Stein's house. Where this orb came from—if it's part of the curse—I don't know. But I do know that it has to be destroyed."

"So if we can't use the bat, what are we going to do?" Darius asks.

Sofia turns around. "Well, it's fairly simple. We push the table over."

"How is that any better?" Regan says, still unable to take her eyes off the deadly lightning. "Won't the charge still be unstable?"

"Once the orb is knocked loose, the electricity should stop, as it doesn't have a base for its power. And pushing it *away* from us will cause it all to go in that direction."

Sofia points to the back wall of Ms. Stein's dining room that has a large cabinet filled with glass and china plates and a few family photos.

"But what about the mess?" Regan asks.

Sofia turns around and glares at her. "*That's* your concern right now? The *mess*?! Do I need to remind you that Ms. Stein is trying to— you know what. How about the fact that your parents will be much more upset with you if our clones keep causing trouble? That all of our families' reputations will be ruined if this doesn't stop. Darius's mother will be out of a job. I doubt my father will be able to run the Visitors Center if his two children are tarnishing Cauldron's Cove's status as a family-friendly tourist destination." Bennett stands a little straighter at Sofia's including him as part of her family for the first time . . . ever. "Not to mention your parents' business, Regan. This is the only way."

Regan pauses for a moment. Sofia has a point (of course she does). Regan has been so focused on disappointing her parents that she didn't think about what will happen if she—Regan Charles, the girl people judge for being fat, for struggling in class—can actually stop this curse. How her parents could look at her with pride again. How maybe, just maybe, she can start doing things for herself for a change.

Regan goes over to the table with a determined look on her face. "Then let's push this over."

"But what about the goo?" Bennett points his bat at the glass container. "Can I destroy that?"

Sofia rolls her eyes. "You'll get a chance to flex your muscles, but first . . ."

Sofia joins Regan at one side of the table and puts her hands on the underside. Darius and Bennett flank them.

"Now, be careful. We'll do it on the count of three. And let's try to not die," Sofia adds casually.

"What?" Regan exclaims before Sofia starts the countdown.

"One."

All four kids plant their feet firmly on the ground.

"Two."

They flex their hands against the table.

"Three."

They lift the table with all their strength.

And . . . nothing.

The table doesn't even budge an inch.

"The electrical current is weighting the table down," Sofia growls. "We don't have the strength to do this on our own."

Bennett's face falls. "What do you mean?"

"No! We can do it! We *have* to do it!" Darius says through gritted teeth as the rest join him in trying to get the table to move. "Come on!"

"Stop!" A scream comes from the front door.

The exhausted foursome turn to find Ms. Stein, with the clones behind her.

Gulp.

"What do you think you're doing?" Ms. Stein screeches.

BANG! BANG! BANG! Pounding comes from the closet, where the monster has been locked in.

Ms. Stein opens the door and the monster rushes out, an angry look on its face.

The four kids are now surrounded.

And outnumbered.

21

So yeah. This isn't good.

Not like anything in this book has been good for the kids so far. But *this*?

Yikes.

The room crackles with lightning.

Regan's body shakes as she takes in a very angry and unhinged Ms. Stein, backed up by one very intimidating monster and four not-as-intimidating-but-still-outnumbering-them clones.

"It's over, Ms. Stein," Sofia says with the confidence of someone *not* trapped. Leave it to Sofia to think they're at an advantage right now. "Your clones are a smelly disaster. Your plan has failed."

Clone Bennett grunts in reply.

"But I do like that one," Sofia says as Real Bennett groans in protest.

The lightning in the room intensifies. Darius holds up his hands to block out the light while Bennett puts on sunglasses, which he carries on him at all times because, as I've said before, he's one cool dude.

Sofia squints at their teacher. "Listen, Ms. Stein, you're probably not aware of this, but you're cursed. In fact, I don't think you have any control over what you're doing. Or even have any idea that you're doing it. Leave it to the one teacher I somewhat enjoy to be—"

Sofia stops as Ms. Stein grabs her hair and runs over to the orb. "What should I do? Have I failed you? Have I disappointed you?" She takes a step back as a loud clap of thunder rattles the entire house. "Well, I was only following *your* plan and you— Excuse me? How dare you! I'm simply doing what I was told. Well, yes, then maybe you should've."

Yep, their science teacher is having a one-sided argument with a metal ball that's shooting lightning.

"I absolutely will not!" Ms. Stein screams at the orb. "You can't make me."

With a giant yelp, Ms. Stein collapses on the floor. She's curled into the fetal position, her hands hitting her head, as if she's trying to fight whatever is going on in her mind. Trying to get *whoever* is in there out of her head.

I think at this point, it's pretty obvious—at least to me—that it just might be Ann Wilder speaking to Ms. Stein through the orb.

"Listen here, Ann Wilder," Darius says to the orb. "You're not welcome here. Leave Ms. Stein and Cauldron's Cove alone!"

"It's over, Ann," Sofia states calmly.

Okay, if Darius and Sofia agree, it has to be the spirit or whatever of the witch who set the curse.

Regan kneels next to Ms. Stein and places her hand on Ms. Stein's shaking shoulders. "It's going to be okay, Ms. Stein. We know this isn't you. We're going to help."

Ms. Stein's eyes roll back in her head before she passes out.

Bennett takes a step toward the table. "We've got to knock this thing over."

"But maybe we should—"

Regan is cut off by an even larger surge of lightning. The room is nearly blindingly white. Suddenly, a gust of wind comes from nowhere, swirling Ms. Stein's pages around the room.

"We don't have time!" Bennett says as he tries to move the table, but it's still too heavy for the four of them.

"We need help!" Darius says as a loud clap of thunder ricochets off the walls.

Sofia approaches the monster and clones who have been blankly watching the scene before them. "You are all being used and you need to be set free." She stands on her tippy-toes in an attempt to look into the monster's beady eyes. "This isn't your fault."

The monster grunts in reply, but it seems soft, almost as if the monster has a tender spot for Sofia.

"Please help us. We need your strength." She looks at the other clones. "We need *all* of you. It's the only way we can defeat the curse. We have to do it together."

The clones and monster stare blankly back.

"I'm not one to ask for help," Sofia admits. "So it would really mean a lot. Please."

Regan apprehensively goes over and holds out her hand to her clone, who studies her hand for a moment before taking it.

"Thanks." Regan gives her clone a smile, at which the clone smiles in return. Which isn't as nice of a sight, as clones apparently aren't into dental hygiene. Clone Regan's teeth are black and rotting. But flossing and mouthwash can wait for another day.

Regan and her clone move to the table and get into position.

Darius goes over to his and does the same. Then Bennett. Then Sofia.

After Sofia's clone is stationed at the table, Sofia approaches the monster. "We need you. *I* need you."

The monster grunts as it takes the center of the table.

Maybe they have a chance to destroy the orb after all.

It's now four students, four clones, and one monster versus a very heavy table and one curse.

"Okay," Sofia calls out. "On the count of three, we need to use all our strength to turn this over and get that orb out of commission. Ready?"

Ms. Stein stirs on the floor. Her eyes blink open as she takes in the scene before her. "No!" she yells in protest.

"Ready," Regan says with a fierce nod.

"Laaaalaaaaalaaaaaaa," Clone Regan sings loudly.

"Ready," Darius says with the confidence of the superheroes he loves so much.

"Gaaaaahhhhh," Darius's clone replies.

"You know I'm so ready, Sof—" Bennett begins.

"It's—" Sofia starts before sighing.

Bennett's face lights up before he turns to his clone. "You ready?"

The clone—*shockingly!*—grunts in reply.

"Good enough for me."

"One . . ." Sofia begins.

All nine beings grip the underside of the table.

"Two . . ." They plant their feet firmly on the ground, ready to put their whole bodies into it.

"Three!"

Everybody—clones and humans alike—groans as they start moving the table up, up, up and—*BOOM!*—over it goes.

Light flashes around them as the orb goes smashing through the glass cabinet on the wall. The lightning flickers on and off wildly, wind whooshing around them. It's like a tornado inside the room; papers are flying around and then . . .

The orb bounces into the corner of the room as it plunges the group into total darkness.

22

"Is everybody okay?" Darius asks into the darkness.

There's glass crunching and some human grunting as Darius blindly feels his way over to the wall to open the curtains. The fall sunshine immediately brightens the room. Darius covers his eyes to give them time to adjust, and when he finally opens them, it is not a good scene.

Broken glass litters the carpet where the table smashed into the cabinet. China plates and glass vases are destroyed. In short, Ms. Stein's dining room is a disaster.

"Be careful," Darius calls out as he cautiously makes his way back to the group.

Ms. Stein sits up from the floor. She blinks a few times. "What—what—what's going on?" she asks in a daze. "Who are . . ." She squints at her four students, their clones, and one very large monster.

"Ah, Ms. Stein? Are you all right?" Darius asks.

"I don't . . . What happened? Why are you . . . Who are they . . ."

Ms. Stein moves her head around like she's hoping something will snap back into place.

"You were cursed," Bennett states bluntly. "I mean, that's what happened, right? She was cursed by Ann Wilder and now . . . it's over?"

"Cursed?" Ms. Stein says as she rubs her head.

"We'll explain everything to you when you're ready," Sofia says in a soft voice, and gives her teacher a small smile.

Regan looks around the chaotic room, her heart still beating wildly. It seems like everything is fine, but . . .

"Is it really over?" Regan asks.

The four study one another and the scene before them. Ms. Stein looks . . . well, not normal, but she's not angry at them. She looks as confused as Regan has felt these last few days. The clones are still alive but standing on unstable feet. Which isn't that different from before.

"I think so," Sofia says.

Ms. Stein curls into herself.

"It's going to be okay, Ms. Stein," Darius reassures her.

"I'm just . . . really . . . tired," she says before closing her eyes.

She's not the only one who needs a nap.

The monster takes a few timid steps back, then stumbles onto the floor with a grunt. The clones sway for a few beats before sitting down in the middle of the mess. It only takes a few seconds before Clone Bennett starts snoring.

Sofia kneels next to the monster. "I think they're losing their strength. The orb is what powered them." She scowls as she takes in this big monster, who she should technically be scared of, but Sofia instead puts her hand tenderly on its cheek. "You helped save us."

"Wait, what's going to happen to them?" Regan asks, a lump forming in her throat. She makes her way to a slumped-over Clone Regan.

It's silly for Regan to be upset over the clone . . . it's not dying, is it? But as she looks at a distorted version of herself, Regan can't help but feel bad. Her clone didn't ask to be part of a plan for world (or at least Cauldron's Cove) domination. The clone didn't do anything wrong.

(Well, there was the whole smashing a window and scaring Regan's younger siblings and getting Regan into all sorts of trouble, but let's not bring that up to her now. Regan's already upset enough as is.)

The room is quiet as the foursome look at their clones, who seem to have lost all their energy.

Then there's a small noise.

Bloop.

What's that?

Bloop. Bloop. Bloop.

The vat of goo is bubbling up.

That can't be good.

(It isn't.)

Sofia approaches the bubbling vat and bends down, examining the goo. "It still has some charge left in it. It's acting like a battery."

"What does that mean?" Darius asks.

"It means that we may have broken the curse, but we still have to get rid of it. We need to empty it or—"

"Okay, it's go time!" Bennett doesn't wait for Sofia to say another word. It's like he's been waiting all day for this moment. And with that excited look on his face as he grips his bat, perhaps he has.

Bennett takes a few steps toward the large vat, which is nearly as tall as him. He pulls back and swings the baseball bat at the glass with all his might.

And . . . *clink*.

The bat ricochets back with such force, Bennett stumbles a bit. There isn't a single mark on the glass container.

Ms. Stein picks her head up. "I don't . . . don't know why I know this, but it has to be destroyed." And with that, Ms. Stein collapses back down and starts snoring loudly.

Poor Ms. Stein hasn't had a proper night's sleep in days. She's going to be out for a while.

"Come on, muscles," Sofia taunts Bennett.

Bennett in return starts swinging at the glass vat.

THWACK. THWACK. THWACK.

And the large glass vessel stubbornly remains intact. The bubbling intensifies.

"Come on!" Darius says as he picks up the second bat to join Bennett in the bashing of the vat.

The goo moves inside and seems to *like* being jostled about. In fact, it's bubbling with delight.

"No! We're so close!" Bennett cries out. "This has to end."

Regan feels so helpless. It's like when she's in class and nothing that's been written on the whiteboard makes any sense. When she tries to understand numbers in math class, but they move around in her mind. When she has trouble pronouncing words aloud and gets laughed at.

"Come on!" Bennett yells as the glass remains intact.

"It has to be destroyed," Sofia says.

Bennett wipes the sweat off his brow. "That's what we're trying to do."

Sofia goes over to the monster, who looks exhausted. Its breathing is shallow, and its skin is even greener. "Can you help?"

The monster gives a quiet, defeated grunt in reply.

Regan balls her fists tightly. All the frustration she's felt the last couple of days starts simmering under her surface, just like the goo. First, she gets put in detention for no reason. Then she gets in trouble with her parents. Now River and Rose are scared of her after the whole clone window incident at day care. Not to mention the small fact that Regan never gets to do what Regan wants to do.

She can't take any more of this.

"Ugh!" Darius exclaims in frustration as he throws his bat down. "It's hopeless."

Regan is tired of being frustrated and feeling like she can't do anything right. She doesn't know what's going to happen when this is over—*if* this will ever be over. But she does know that she's done feeling sorry for herself. Of sitting back and pretending to be fine doing what others want instead of what Regan wants.

What Regan wants more than anything is to end this. *Now*.

"It is *not* hopeless," Regan finds herself saying.

Before she can think it through, she walks over to the vat. She picks up Darius's bat off the floor. Her entire body is pulsating with energy. She closes her eyes and lets all the frustration she's ever felt build inside her.

Regan opens her eyes, grips the bat, and doesn't hold back as she crashes it against the glass.

The tiniest crack appears on the surface.

"There's a weak spot!" Sofia exclaims.

"I am *not* weak!" Regan screams as she hits the glass container again.

And again.

The tiny crack starts splintering.

And one more time.

THWACK!

The bat makes contact with the glass and splits through the container. The gloopy, green goo splashes across the room, drenching everybody—and everything—in the dining room.

Regan looks at the bat in her hand. She can't believe she did it. Regan has destroyed the vat. She has saved the day.

But *whoa*, does this stuff smell, and now it's *everywhere*.

"Ugh," Bennett exclaims as he wipes the goo out of his hair and mouth. "My hair!"

"It's an improvement," Sofia replies.

Darius's nose scrunches up as he takes in the stink. He lifts up his Falcon T-shirt to get the goo out of his face and nostrils.

Sofia studies the goo in her hand. Every surface of Ms. Stein's destroyed living room is covered in the snot-colored stuff. "Well, that went well," she remarks dryly.

But see, it *did* go well! The curse has been lifted from a very confused Ms. Stein! The orb and goo are destroyed!

I mean, there's one person this hasn't gone well for at all, and she has seemed to wake up from her power nap.

Ms. Stein blinks in her destroyed room and wipes the green goo off her face and arms and legs. "Children, what on earth happened?"

Bennett looks down at his science teacher and the very drained-looking clones. "Ah . . ."

Everybody turns to Sofia.

"What are we supposed to do now?" Darius asks the others under his breath. "I mean, are we really supposed to tell everybody what she did? It isn't her fault she was cursed. She wasn't in control of what happened."

Ms. Stein looks confused. "What . . . ?" She glances around, and it's as if she's seeing the clones for the first time. "Oh my. Did I . . . ?" And then Ms. Stein faints.

"Ms. Stein!" Regan calls out as she kneels next to her teacher. "What are we going to do? If we turn her in . . ."

What Regan doesn't want to say is that if they tell on Ms. Stein, they'll get out of trouble. Her parents won't be so disappointed in her. Her siblings will know that she's not some window-smashing monster. She might get to finally take a deep breath.

That is, *if* anyone believes them. And that's a very big *if*.

Bennett walks over to Sofia, trying not to slide on the slippery, gooey floor. "We have to turn her in. It's the only way to clear our names. Right, Sof?"

"It's Sofia." She grimaces as she takes in the messy room and the fading clones. "Actually, I have a different idea."

23

Walking down the hallway of Cauldron's Cove Elementary is a totally normal, nearly daily occurrence for Regan.

But today feels different.

Regan has a secret.

They all do: Regan, Darius, Sofia, Bennett, *and* Ms. Stein.

And now Regan's expected to go back to life as normal. Is that even possible?

Here's something you should know about *me*: I know that I am forever changed by the incidents in this book. I'll never look at a science teacher or snot the same way again.

"Hey, Regan!" Darius calls out as he falls in step next to her. "How did last night go with your parents?"

"It was okay," Regan says, even though it was anything but. She had to apologize to her parents and pretend that *she* was the one who smashed the window *and* that she got detention for talking in class, even though it's not true. "I have to give the day care half of my allowance until the window is paid off *and* I'm grounded for two weeks. You?"

"Yeah, it was rough." Darius shakes his head. "But I know my mom, so before she ordered me to write apology notes—she's a big fan of handwritten letters—I offered to bake each person that was in the town square brownies, cookies, whatever they'd like and hand deliver the treat *and* a verbal apology. Mom liked that personal touch, so hopefully it won't come up during the campaign."

"That's really nice of you."

Darius shrugs. "I like baking, but it stings that my mom might have trouble because of something I *didn't* do. But when you really think about it, I wouldn't believe it if anybody told me that . . ."

He doesn't need to finish that thought. Besides, Darius has a point. To be honest, *I* wouldn't believe what happened, either, if I hadn't written it.

"Yeah." Regan nods along.

The heroes decided it was easier to say sorry, take their punishments, and move on.

"Yo!" Bennett calls down from the hallway. He jogs over to Darius and Regan. "Come on, Sof!"

"It's Sofia," Sofia replies with a scowl as she joins them.

"How's Ms. Stein?" Regan asks.

"She's better. She's taking time off work, saying it's the flu." Sofia looks over at Ms. Stein's classroom, where a substitute teacher sits at her desk. "Plus, it's going to take a while for her to get that goo out of the carpet."

"I can't believe she doesn't remember anything," Darius comments. "I mean, I'm just grateful she's not blaming us for what happened to her room."

"Even though it *is* our fault," Regan adds, because it's true.

Bennett scoffs in a way that is very Sofia. "Well, if she didn't try to—"

"But *she* didn't," Darius reminds him. "It was the curse."

"And the clones?" Regan asks, worried about what has happened to her clone. There's also a part of her that doesn't want to know. The clones and monster were all so weak after the orb and goo were destroyed.

"I've taken care of it" is all Sofia will say on the subject.

Which is probably for the best, even though I'm a bit curious. *Girls and their secrets, am I right?*

"Our parents are so mad at us for everything," Bennett says.

"Yeah," Darius and Regan reply at the same time. They look at each other and smile.

Even though it was very stressful and scary, Regan likes that she has something between her and Darius. And Sofia. And yes, even Bennett.

The four kids pause in the hallway. They have a bond now, a secret that only they know.

Maybe this is even the start of a beautiful friendship?

"So yeah," Darius says as he nods his head. "Ah, I've got to get to class. So I guess I'll see you all around."

"Yo, B-man!" Bennett's friend Jimmy calls out. "You wearing deodorant today, dude?" He then waves his hand in front of his nose.

Bennett grimaces. "I don't even want to know what my clone did yesterday, but ah . . . I'll catch you later!"

"Yeah, later," Darius replies.

Then Darius and Bennett head in opposite directions.

"Oh, okay," Regan says quietly to their backs. Can they really just move on from what happened so easily? Maybe they aren't friends, after all. Will Bennett even talk to her in front of his friends or will he be embarrassed like he was in the library? And here she thought they shared a nice moment in the tree house.

"So . . ." Regan starts to say to Sofia, who is standing awkwardly in the hallway.

"Yeah, I guess . . ." Sofia pauses for a second.

Wait a second. Does *Sofia Vargas* also want friends?

Whenever Regan saw Sofia by herself in the cafeteria or annoyed because Bennett asked her to do things or dismissive when Darius invited her to lunch, Regan assumed it's because Sofia wants to be alone.

But who would want to live a life without friends?

Regan knows in her heart that she wants to be friends with her detention-mates.

Regan wants it so much.

Sofia opens her mouth for a second before snapping it shut. "Bye," she says abruptly before turning around.

"Wait!" Regan calls out.

Sofia twirls around, an annoyed (*shocking!*) expression on her face. "What is it?"

Ask her to join you at lunch, Regan wills herself. *Or ask her to come over after school.*

But who would really want to watch Regan wrangle her siblings and do chores and . . . ?

Instead Regan asks, "Is it really over?"

As much as Regan wants to be done with Ann Wilder's curse, she doesn't want to be done with Sofia, Bennett, and Darius.

"Of course," Sofia replies bluntly, but there's a slight pause before she walks away.

Hmm . . . maybe Sofia wanted to be asked to do something non-homework and non-curse related?

Regan's shoulders slump. So that's it. Regan should be relieved. Everything is back to normal.

It seems the Cauldron's Cove curse has indeed been broken.

. . . OR HAS IT?

A few nights later, a fog rolls into the Cauldron's Cove Cemetery. Moonlight shines down at the gravestones that are hundreds of years old, with old-timey names like Gertrude, Elmer, Herbert, Bertha, *Elizabeth* . . .

There's a weird charge in the air. Something seems to be moving near one of the gravestones.

Is it a squirrel? A rat? A very large worm?

Let's take a closer look, shall we?

There's some green grass, fallen autumn leaves. Everything looks completely as one would expect for a cemetery.

Then—*BAM!*—a hand pops up from the dirt. Its skin is falling away, bones poking out from the fingertips.

Uh-oh.

Did you *really* think the curse was over?

ACKNOWLEDGMENTS

Dear reader, you may think that I, your lovable and adorable narrator, did this entire book on my own. I mean, I am super smart and talented and above all extremely, *extremely* humble. Alas, just like our heroes of this story, I didn't work alone. I can assure you that the following people do *not* have evil lairs and *do* smell fantastic. (But then again, I told you never to trust a ginger.)

First, my apologies to my wonderful editor, Talia Seidenfeld, for this book being such a nightmare to work on. Not because of me (because as we know, I'm *delightful*), but due to any nightmares, sickening-stomach feelings, and tremors this story may have caused. Thank you for being such a champion for this story and the Cauldron's Cove Crew. I'll go easier on you next time. (Spoiler alert: I won't!)

My life would be utterly terrifying without David Levithan. Friend, shoulder to snot on, mentor, publishing demon. Did I say demon? *Oops*. (Don't worry, David, your secret for world domination is safe with me!) But for reals, my friend, I'd take a baseball bat to protect you from a witch's curse any day.

No nightmares for me at night with Suzie Townsend and the team at New Leaf Literary having my back. Thank you for believing in this from the first email of *Hey, so I have an idea* . . . Extra big thanks to Kate Sullivan, Sophia Ramos, and Kendra Coet.

Like a warm blanket and being covered in goo, it feels so good to be back home. Thank you to the amazing team at Scholastic for welcoming me back with open arms and terrifying screams, especially, Jackie Dever, Mary Kate Garmire, Stephanie Yang, Priscilla Eakleley, and Maya Marlette. And of course to the legal department for having to put me in line when I ███████████████████████████████.

Thank you, Eloise Szaruga-Bolt, for this incredible cover art.

If I ever have to defeat some curse, I know that I have a wonderful group of ragtag author friends who are just a text or Zoom chat away. First, James Ponti, who read a very, *very* rough draft and sprinkled it with so much awesomeness (and realized the town of Cauldron's Cove could be so much more—totally going to race you on the Broom Broom Speedway, James!). Jen Calonita, my ride or die, who is there when I need her the most. Um, Jen, you're going to need to read this under the covers. Sorry. (Not sorry.) Through lockdowns and a move to another country, I could always count on Sarah Mlynowski,

Christina Soontornvat, Stuart Gibbs, Max Brallier, Gordon Korman, Julie Buxbaum, and Rose Brock for a fun chat and a séance or fifteen. Not that authors are evil. Well, *some* aren't.

While this book contained a possessed teacher, I possess only awe and admiration for teachers, librarians, and educators. As someone who shares the same learning differences as Regan, I wouldn't be this (awesome, talented, and again, *humble*) author without the support of the educators in my life, especially my librarian mother. I was never defined by my learning issues and was allowed to dream as big as possible. I mean, LOOK AT ME NOW, MOM! *And yes, I plan on taking a shower at some point today. Jeez.*

Last, but not least, to you, dear smart, wonderful, gorgeous-on-the-inside-and-out reader. Thank you for picking up this book. For ignoring the warning at the beginning and getting through to the very end. For telling every single person you meet—or heck, anybody you *see*—that they need to buy this book *immediately*. (If you haven't done that yet, it's okay, I can wait . . . Done? Great! You da best!) This is just the start for this crew. I (make no) promise to have the next story be not as scary or silly.

Again, never trust a ginger. Mmmmwaaaaahaaaaahaaaaaaaaa.

CAN'T GET ENOUGH SILLY SCARES?
THE STORY CONTINUES IN

KEEP READING FOR A SNEAK PEEK!

There have been rumors around town about weird things happening at the cemetery. Darius's mom was on her phone all through dinner even though there's a no-phones / no-screen rule in the Washington household during meals.

Why don't the rules apply to *her*?

So. Not. Fair.

Darius's mother has been locked in her home office all evening. His dad has been sent out to meet with his staff at Broom Broom Speedway, Cauldron's Cove's popular go-kart track. There were—

Okay, I know you got a warning at the beginning, and I just told you in the last chapter to go back and read it, but I really, *really* feel you need to know that if you're squeamish, you should brace yourself. Or if you've just eaten, you may want to wait like fifteen minutes before continuing.

I'm serious. Dead serious.

Okay, consider yourself triple warned.

Mr. Washington had to have an emergency meeting because the racetrack was littered with mostly eaten dead squirrels. Their heads were completely gone.

Yup. *Barf.*

So! Are you now going to believe your trusty and benevolent and totes adorbs narrator when she warns you in the future?

Good.

So yeah, Darius has his ear pressed against his mother's door, and what he's hearing is bad. Really, *really* bad.

"Every year it's the same thing, but this is on a whole other level." His mother's voice is strained. "The cemetery is a mess. For the last two nights, a grave has been dug up. Dirt is everywhere. I don't even want to think about where the bodies could be. This is just so unsettling . . ."

A chill runs down Darius's spine. Bodies missing in the cemetery is not a good sign.

But his mother isn't done yet.

"We have to find that tour group that's gone missing. But we must keep this quiet. We can't let people think it's not safe to come to Cauldron's Cove."

Okay, this is probably a good time to give you a little reminder about Cauldron's Cove. While the town may have forgotten about

Ann Wilder and what they did to her, it loves embracing witches in a punny and money-making way. Tourists are invited to "stay a spell" in the picturesque town for its many events—including the aforementioned Zombie 5K—and the Witches' Way main street is filled with businesses like Hocus Focus Photography Studio, Witches Brew and SandWitch Shop, and Bubble Bubble Toil and Trouble. So it's important that the town keep up its family-friendly reputation.

And guess whose number one job it is to keep it that way?

You got it.

Darius's mom continues. "Whatever is happening, we've got to keep it under wraps. October is our biggest month, and businesses downtown are relying on our influx of tourists. We can't have anything that will scare them away."

It's quiet for a bit. Darius's eyes are moving back and forth like he's doing some complicated calculation on what he's hearing.

His mom starts talking again, "I know, it's the same thing that happened with Michael at the track, but pigs at the Talbot farm? What kind of animal has the capability to cause this much destruction? Have you heard anything about bears in the area?"

"Empty graves, people missing, animals being eaten . . ." Darius says to himself. He takes a quick breath as he steps away from the door.

It's like Darius is living in one of the comic books he loves to read. And unfortunately, this one isn't about superheroes. It's about creatures that come back from the dead and feed on flesh.

"We need more help, Captain Rodgers," his mother says, her voice getting louder. "Our budget for security is already strained with this weekend's Zombie 5K and all our other events—"

Darius backs away from the door, but his mother is still talking, stressed out about budgets and security. "I've got to tell her," he says to himself as he puts his hand on the doorknob, but then he pulls it away.

Just like Regan, Bennett, and Sofia, Darius is also still in big trouble from the clone shenanigans. His mother thinks he and Sofia caused chaos in the town square and ruined a bunch of picnics, but again, it wasn't Darius and Sofia. It was their *clones*. As the mayor's son, Darius has extra pressure on him to behave and always do the right thing.

He can't tell his mother that it's—

He can hardly say the word.

Not like his mother would believe him.

Not like *any* adult would believe him.

Darius's face lights up. He knows three people that definitely would.